Her cheeks were [...]
to the shock of fi[...]
noticed what she was holding.

A baby.

Wrapped toe to neck in some kind of zip-up covering, all Jake could see of the child were big blue eyes—just like his own.

A jolt of emotions shot through him so hard he gripped the doorknob tight to keep from falling over in shock.

"What the hell?"

"Jake," Cassie said, "meet your son. Luke."

"My *son?*" Silently, Jake congratulated himself on the control keeping his voice from raging with the fury erupting inside him.

He couldn't believe this. For a year and a half, this woman had haunted him, waking and sleeping. Hell, he'd hardly known her and shouldn't have given her another thought once she was gone. But he had.

He'd even fantasized a couple times about seeing her here again.

He just had never imagined her carrying his child along with her.

His child. He had a son.

* * *

The Cowboy's Pride and Joy is part of the #1 bestselling miniseries from Harlequin Desire—Billionaires & Babies: Powerful men...wrapped around their babies' little fingers.

* * *

If you're on Twitter,
tell us what you think of Harlequin Desire!
#harlequindesire

Cassie was back.

Dear Reader,

I love to read—and write—books set at Christmas. There's something so inherently joyful about that time of year that it doesn't seem to matter what holiday we happen to be celebrating. It's about family. And love. And taking the time to be with the ones important to us—and a little time for ourselves.

In *The Cowboy's Pride and Joy,* you'll meet Jake Hunter and Cassidy Moore. Jake hasn't celebrated Christmas in years. He's cut himself off from his family, as well. So when Cassidy starts dragging him back to the land of the living, he fights her every step of the way. I really enjoyed writing this book, and I hope you'll love it, too!

And, whatever holiday you're celebrating, I wish you joy and laughter and really good books! Come and see me on Facebook, and check out my website at www.maureenchild.com.

Maureen

THE COWBOY'S PRIDE AND JOY

—

MAUREEN CHILD

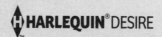 HARLEQUIN® DESIRE

Recycling programs
for this product may
not exist in your area.

ISBN-13: 978-0-373-73348-4

The Cowboy's Pride and Joy

Copyright © 2014 by Maureen Child

Printed in U.S.A.

www.Harlequin.com

MAUREEN CHILD

writes for the Harlequin Desire line and can't imagine a better job. Being able to indulge your love for romance, as well as being able to spin stories just the way you want them told, is—in a word—perfect.

A seven-time finalist for the prestigious Romance Writers of America RITA® Award, Maureen is the author of more than one hundred romance novels. Her books regularly appear on the bestseller lists and have won several awards, including a Prism, a National Readers' Choice Award, a Colorado Romance Writers Award of Excellence and a Golden Quill.

One of her books, *The Soul Collector,* was made into a CBS TV movie starring Melissa Gilbert, Bruce Greenwood and Ossie Davis. If you look closely, in the last five minutes of the movie, you'll spot Maureen, who was an extra in the last scene.

Maureen believes that laughter goes hand in hand with love, so her stories are always filled with humor. The many letters she receives assure her that her readers love to laugh as much as she does.

Maureen Child is a native Californian, but has recently moved to the mountains of Utah. She loves a new adventure, though the thought of having to deal with snow for the first time is a little intimidating.

This book is dedicated to my grand-dog, Bristow. Funny, sweet, loyal, Bristow loves with his whole heart and we're so glad to have him in our family.

One

"When Boston comes to Montana, it's never a good thing." Jake Hunter frowned into the distance.

"You always were too hard on your mother."

Jake turned his head to look at the older man standing beside him. At seventy-five years old, Ben Hawkins didn't stand as straight and tall as he once had. But he still had a full head of snow-white hair, piercing blue eyes, and a face weathered and tanned from years of working in the sun.

"And you were always too soft on her."

Ben shrugged that away with a half smile. "She's my daughter."

"There is that." Jake nodded. "Anyway, if it all goes as promised, this will be the last time Boston comes calling for anything but a family visit."

"I've got to ask. Are you sure about this?" Ben

pulled the collar of his coat up higher around his neck against the cold autumn wind. "I mean, what you're planning can't be changed. You're signing away your rights to the business your family built."

"Oh," Jake assured him, "I'm sure. This has been a long time coming, Pop." Jake shook his head. "Hunter Media has nothing I want. Never has."

And he knew how much that fact irritated his mother. She had always planned on Jake taking over the day-to-day running of the company built by her husband's family. The fact that Jake had never been interested really hadn't bothered her any. Elise Hawkins Hunter was nothing if not determined.

Ben snorted a laugh. "You always were more stubborn than anything else."

"Not stubborn." Jake took a deep breath, relishing the sharp, cold sting that hit his lungs. "I just know what I want. Always have."

Now he glanced around at the ranch he loved. The place that had been his solace and comfort when he'd come here during the summer as a kid—and when he'd returned here after leaving the military.

October in the mountains of Montana was spectacular. As though God was putting on a show just before the winter cold settled in. The trees were turning brilliant shades of gold, orange and red. Dark clouds scudded across a sky so wide and blue it almost hurt your eyes to look at it. From the corral and barn came the sounds of horses and the men working with them. And spilling out in front of and below the huge ranch house he'd built was Whitefish Lake, sapphire water surrounded by tall pines that dipped and swayed with the wind.

The view soothed the dark places inside him, just as it had from the first time he'd seen it as a kid. Jake had known even then that *this* was his place. Not Boston, where he was born and where his family created and ruled a dynasty. But here on the mountain where his grandfather had carved out a way of life that spoke to Jake's soul in a way that nothing else ever had.

"No," he murmured, gaze still locked on the lake below. "Boston has nothing to offer me that can compete with this place."

"Have to say I agree," Ben mused. "Though your mother never did feel the bone-deep connection to the land that you and I do."

That simple statement made Jake smile. Maybe a love of the land skipped generations, he thought. This ranch had been in Ben's family for more than a hundred years, always falling to the oldest child to maintain the legacy the Hawkinses had built since the first settler stumbled into Montana and staked a claim to the land. Until, Jake thought, his mother.

Elise Hawkins Hunter hadn't felt the pull of the ranch. His mother had been born and raised here, and she had escaped as soon as she was able. Going to college in Boston, she'd met and married Jake's father there and settled into the kind of life she'd dreamed of. No early mornings to take care of animals. No quiet stillness. No solitude when the ranch was snowed in.

She'd made plenty of trips to the ranch to visit her parents and sent Jake and his sister out here for a few weeks every summer, but Boston was her home as the ranch had never been.

Elise was still puzzled by her son's decision to walk away from moneyed sophistication in favor of hard work and empty spaces. But Jake had his own money—a fortune he'd built through good investments and well-chosen risks. He didn't need to enslave himself to a desk to get his share of Hunter Media.

His mother might not ever understand his decision, but she had at least, finally, accepted it.

"So when's your mother's assistant due to arrive?"

Jake glanced at his grandfather. "Sometime today, and with any luck, by tomorrow she'll be on her way back to Boston."

"Shame she had to fly all the way here to have you sign papers you could have faxed in."

"You know Mom. A stickler for details." Jake shook his head and hopped off the fence, his battered brown boots sinking into the soft dirt of the corral. "She wants the papers notarized and the assistant's a notary."

"Handy," Ben said. "But then, your mom's always been a thorough one."

Thorough. And stubborn. There was a part of Jake that still didn't believe his mother had given up on luring him back to Boston. But whether she had or not didn't really matter, did it? He wasn't going anywhere. Montana was his home. His sanctuary. Damned if he'd give it up.

Cassidy Moore's hands hurt after an hour of gripping the steering wheel tightly enough to make her knuckles white. Driving up a mountain was more harrowing than she would have thought. Maybe if the narrow road had been straight rather than curved with the occasional sharp right-angle turn, it wouldn't have been so bad. But those curves were there and so was the steep drop off the left side.

If she had known the kind of drive she was letting herself in for, she would have tried to rent a tank at the airport in Kalispell rather than the four-wheel-drive sedan she was currently driving.

"But then," she told herself, "a tank never would have fit on this road."

Seriously. The people who built the darn road couldn't have made it a *little* wider? Every time another car came toward her, she winced in anticipation of a horrific crash. The only good thing about this drive was that it wasn't the dead of winter. "Imagine dealing with this road in snow!"

Just the thought of that gave her cold chills. Ordinarily, she probably would have enjoyed this drive through the mountains, with the bright splashes of fall color on either side of her. But the threat of imminent death sort of took the fun out of it.

Cassidy was out of her element and she knew it. Born and raised in Boston, she had never been west of the Massachusetts border. She was used to busy highways, crowded streets and stoplights every block. In her world, tall buildings created shadowy canyons in the city and the sound of honking horns ensured there was never any quiet to be found. Still, she'd be fine. She was only here for the night, and tomorrow she'd be flying back to Boston with the signed paperwork her boss needed.

She pulled off the narrow road and followed a graveled drive up a sharp incline. When she came out from beneath the arch of trees, she simply stopped the car, turned off the engine and stared.

My son refuses to leave his little ranch, her boss had said. *So you'll have to go to him and get these papers signed.*

Little ranch.

Shaking her head, Cassidy got out of the car, her heels shifting precariously on the gravel beneath her feet. She did a slow turn in place, letting her gaze sweep across her surroundings before finally coming back to land on the "little ranch." There was nothing little about it. Granted, the only experience Cassidy had with ranches was what she'd seen on late-night movies. But this was no ordinary place. Jake Hunter's home was a mountain palace.

Two stories tall, the main house was wood and glass, with floor-to-ceiling windows on each story that would provide a wide view of the lake below. Pine trees huddled close to the house, so that it looked as though it was actually a part of the landscape rather than an intrusion. There were other, smaller houses scattered across the property, no doubt for the employees who worked here. *Lucky them,* Cassidy thought, since she couldn't imagine driving up and down that mountain every day for her commute. "Hello, young lady."

Surprised at the deep voice coming from directly behind her, Cassidy spun around so quickly, one of her heels caught on the gravel and her balance went wobbly. The older man snapped one hand out to take her arm to steady her.

"Didn't mean to startle you," he said, giving her a slow smile.

He was in his seventies, but his eyes were sharp and clear and his skin was like old leather from years spent in the sun. His smile was warm and the chuckle beneath his words was kind.

"Sorry," she said, holding one hand out. "I didn't hear you come up. I'm Cassidy Moore."

He took her hand in his and gave it a firm shake. "You're Elise's new assistant." Nodding, he added, "I'm her father, Ben Hawkins."

"She has your eyes."

His smile got wider. "My eyes, but thankfully she got everything else from her mother, God rest her." He took a step back and said, "You're here to see my grandson."

"Yes," she said, grateful for the quick change of subject. "I've got some papers for him to look over and sign…"

"My daughter's a fiend for paperwork," he said, then waved one hand. "Come along with me, I'll take you to Jake."

She glanced at her car, thinking about her purse lying on the front seat, but then she realized that this wasn't Boston and a purse snatcher wasn't going to reach in and grab anything. So she followed Ben Hawkins, taking careful steps that didn't come close to matching his long, even strides.

Cassidy had dressed to impress and now that it was too late, she was rethinking that. She wore black slacks, a white dress shirt and a cardinal-red waist-length jacket. Her black heels added an extra three inches to her measly five-foot-four frame, and in the city that gave her extra confidence. Here, walking on gravel, she could only wish for the sneakers tucked into the bottom of her bag.

But first impressions counted, and she'd wanted to

come across as sleek and professional to her boss's son. So she'd find a way to maneuver over tricky ground and make it look good while she was doing it.

"It's a beautiful place," she said.

"It is that," the older man agreed, slowing his steps a bit. "I lived my whole life here, but in the few years Jake's been in charge he's made so many changes sometimes I look around and can't believe what he's done in so short a time."

She looked at him. "You sound pleased by that."

"Oh, I am." He winked at her. "I know most old men don't care much for change. But far as I'm concerned, if you're not changing, you're dead. So when Jake came to Montana for good, I turned over the ranch to him and said, 'Do what you want.'" Chuckling again, he added, "He took me up on it."

Smiling, she decided she liked Ben Hawkins.

"He started right out building the new ranch house," Ben said, waving one hand at the spectacular building on their left. "Designed it himself and even did a lot of the construction on his own, too."

"It's beautiful," she said, throwing another glance at the gorgeous house.

"It is," he agreed. "Too much house for a man on his own, though."

"On his own?" She frowned a little. "Don't you live there, too?"

Ben laughed. "No, I live there."

He pointed at one of the smaller buildings, and she noted that it did look older, somehow more *settled,* than the newer structures around it.

"It's the original ranch house and for me, it's home."

They approached a corral and Ben took her elbow

to steady her as she stepped off the gravel onto soft dirt. Her heels sank and she grimaced, but her gaze was caught on the cowboy riding a big black horse around the interior of the corral.

The cowboy looked as comfortable in the saddle as she was in a desk chair. Animal and man moved as one and Cassidy stepped closer to the rail fence, mesmerized as she watched their progress. There was a cold wind blowing, yet she hardly noticed the chill as she kept her gaze fixed on the man on the horse.

"That's my grandson, Jake," Ben told her. "I'll let him know you're here."

Ben walked off but Cassidy didn't see him go. Instead, she studied the cowboy even more closely. And she realized why it was that her boss hadn't been able to convince her son to move to the city. A man that at home on a horse would never be happy in a city of concrete and cars. Even from a distance there was a wildness to him that intrigued her even as her mind whispered for caution. After all, she wasn't here to admire her boss's son. This visit was not only going to be brief, but strictly business as well. Which didn't mean, she assured herself silently, that she couldn't admire the view.

Ben whistled, sharp and short. Jake looked up, then looked to Cassidy when his grandfather pointed her out. She saw his features tighten and she told herself it didn't matter. But as he rode closer to her, she took a single step back from the corral fence.

Were all horses that big?

Jake Hunter swung down and leaned his forearm on the top rail of the fence even as he rested the toe of one battered boot on the bottom rung. Cassidy swallowed hard. Close up, he was even more intriguing.

Black hair, mostly hidden beneath his hat, curled over the collar of his brown leather jacket. His eyes were so blue and so hard, they looked like chips of ice. Black beard stubble covered his jaws and his mouth was thinned into a straight line. His jeans were faded and worn, and over them, he wore a pair of soft, light brown chaps that seemed to hug what looked like *very* long, muscular legs.

A swirl of something warm and intimate rushed through her and Cassidy took a deep, deliberate breath of the cold mountain air, hoping it would help. It really didn't.

"You're not what I was expecting," he said and his voice was a low rumble.

She could have said, *yeah, same to you.* But she didn't. This was ridiculous. She was here to do a job. This was her boss's *son* for heaven's sake, and standing there ogling him like an idiot was so not the kind of impression she had planned to make.

"Well, I'm pleased to meet you anyway," she finally said and held out one hand.

He glanced at her outstretched palm for a long second or two, then reached through the fence and took her hand in his. An instant zing of electricity shot up her arm to settle in her chest and send her heartbeat into a wild, hard gallop. *Oh my. Only here for ten minutes and I am using horse metaphors.*

Releasing her, Jake took off his hat and speared his fingers through his hair. Which only made things a little worse for Cassidy because really, did he have to have such beautiful, thick, shiny hair?

"Mike!" His shout jolted her out of her thoughts, thank heaven. When another man answered, Jake called out, "Take care of Midnight, will you? I've got some business to see to."

"Sure thing, boss," the man said.

"Midnight's your horse?"

"That's right," Jake told her just before he climbed over the corral fence to jump to the ground right beside her.

There went that little warm bubble of something dangerous, she thought and tried to get a grip. She was not the kind of woman to idly daydream about a gorgeous man. Usually. Jake Hunter seemed to be an exception. He was so tall, she felt dwarfed as he loomed over her, even counting her heels, which were now slipping farther and farther into the dirt.

Frowning, he looked down, then met her eyes and asked, "You wore high heels? To a ranch?"

"Is that a problem?"

"Not for me." A ghost of a smile curved his mouth so briefly, she couldn't be sure it had actually been there at all. Then he turned and headed to the house.

She watched him go, those long legs of his striding purposefully across the graveled drive. He never looked back. Didn't bother to help her as his grandfather had. She opened her mouth to shout after him, but snapped it shut before she could. Fuming silently, Cassidy drew first one heel then the other out of the dirt and started clumsily to the ranch house. Her first impression had gone fabulously badly. Now he thought she was an idiot for not dressing appropriately.

Well, that was fine, because she thought he was a troll for walking off and leaving her when he knew darn well that walking across that gravel in heels was practically a competitive sport. *So much for those warm, intimate thoughts,* she told herself. For a woman to have a decent fantasy going, the hero of said fantasy had to at least be civil.

Which seemed like too much to expect from Jake Hunter.

Jake headed straight for the great room and the wet bar. Usually it would be too early to have a drink, but today was different. Today, he had looked into a pair of cool fog-gray eyes and felt a stirring of something he hadn't even thought about in more than two years. Hell, if he'd had his way he *never* would have felt that deep-down heated tickle of anticipation again.

The only other time he'd ever experienced anything like it had led to a marriage made in hell.

"Good times," he muttered, and tossed his hat to the nearest chair. He shot a quick look out the wide front windows to the sprawl of gravel and grass beyond the glass. Damn woman was still coming, heading to the house with short, wobbly steps that almost made him feel guilty for leaving her to manage on her own.

Almost. Yeah, he could've helped her across the uneven ground, but he would have had to touch her and that buzz of something hot and complicated was still fresh enough in his mind that he didn't want to risk repeating it.

"I didn't ask her to come here," he whispered and poured a shot of Irish whiskey into a crystal tumbler. Lifting the glass, he drank that shot down in one gulp and let the fire in its wake burn away whatever he might have felt if he were any other man.

His gaze fixed on her through the window. Behind her, the wide sky was filling with heavy gray clouds that could bring rain or snow. You just never knew in Montana. Wind lifted her dark blond hair off her shoulders and threw it into a wild halo around her head. Her short red jacket clung to impressive breasts and stopped right at her narrow waist. Her black slacks whipped in the wind, outlining her legs—short but definitely curvy—and those stupid high heels wobbled with every step.

A city girl. Just like the last woman he'd allowed into his life. And even as his body felt interest surge, his mind shrieked for some semblance of sanity. Why in the hell would he let himself be interested in the same kind of woman who had carved out a chunk of his soul not so long ago?

He thought about pouring another drink, then decided against it as his mother's gofer finally made her way onto the porch steps and followed him into the house.

"Mr. Hunter?"

"In here." He heard those heels first, tapping against the bamboo flooring, and as those relentless taps came closer, he stepped out from behind the oak bar to meet her.

She paused in the open, arched doorway and he watched as her gaze swept the room. He saw the pleasure and the approval in her eyes and felt a quick jolt of pride. When he moved to the ranch permanently, he'd wanted to build a new, bigger ranch house. Something that would house the whole family when they came to visit. Something that would mark the land as *his*. He wanted this place stamped as his, and Jake's grandfather had given him free rein.

He'd done a good job on this house. He'd designed it himself, working with an architect to build just the right place—something that would look as though it had always been standing here, in the forest. He had wanted to bring the outdoors in and he had been pleased with the results.

The support beams had been built to look like tree trunks. The windows between those beams showcased the lake below them and the miles of open country, forest and sky that made Montana the best place in the world to live. Dark brown leather couches and chairs were arranged around the huge open space, and a riverstone fireplace stood on the far wall, flames inside the hearth dancing and snapping as a sharp wind chased across the top of the chimney.

"Wow," she said, stepping slowly into the room. "Just…wow."

"Thanks." He smiled in spite of everything, enjoying her reaction to the home he loved. "Pretty great, I admit."

"Oh," she said, shaking her head as she turned in place, taking in everything, "it's better than great. It's so gorgeous I'm even going to forgive you for being a jerk and leaving me out there to make it into the house on my own."

Surprised, he snorted a laugh. "Jerk? Is that the way to talk to your boss's son?"

Cool gray eyes slid over him. "I have a feeling she wouldn't blame me."

He thought about it, imagining his mother's reaction to how he'd left her assistant standing in the yard, and had to wince. "No. Probably not."

"Is there some reason in particular that you're not happy to see me?" she asked. "Or is it women in general you disapprove of?"

One corner of Jake's mouth quirked. "Let's answer that with another question. Are you always this forthright?"

"Usually," she said, nodding. "But I probably shouldn't be. So maybe we should consider ourselves on even ground and start over. Deal?"

He looked at her for a long moment and tried not to notice that her eyes were the very color of the fog that lifted off the surface of the lake. Or that her hair looked soft and tumbled, as if she'd just rolled out of bed. Damn, it really had been too long since he'd had a woman.

"All right," he agreed, to end his train of thought before it went even more astray of the subject at hand. "Deal. Now, you've got some papers for me to look over and sign, correct?"

"Yes. They're in my bag in the car."

She actually turned as if to go lurching out across the gravel again to retrieve her bags. Jake stopped her by saying, "One of the guys will bring your stuff in. You're probably beat from the flying and the drive up the mountain…"

"Actually," she admitted, "I would love a shower and change of clothes."

Oh, he wasn't going to think about her in the shower. He'd been prepared for her to spend the night, though. It was a two-hour drive from the airport, and by the time he finished going over the papers before signing them it would be too dark for her to safely drive down the mountain. So she'd be here overnight and gone in the morning. The earlier the better.

"My housekeeper has your room ready for you," he said abruptly. Leading her across the room, he pointed to the staircase directly opposite the front door. "At the top of the stairs, turn right. Third door on your left."

"Okay," she said, already heading for the stairs. "And thanks."

"Dinner's at seven," he told her. "So come down whenever you're ready."

She laid one hand on the heavily carved banister and turned her head to spear him with one long look. "I'll see you in an hour. We can go over the paperwork before dinner."

"Fine." Good idea. Remember that this was all business. His mother hadn't sent him a woman to warm his bed. She'd sent her assistant here to finally give Jake what he'd wanted for years. Freedom from the Hunter family conglomerate.

Freedom to live his life the way he wanted.

The fact that his mother's messenger was more than he'd expected…well, that wouldn't matter once she was gone.

Two

A few minutes later, Cassidy was trying to relax in a bedroom fit for a queen. She was tired, and she wanted a shower and something to eat. But first, she grabbed her cell phone and checked for coverage. Not surprising to find that she was good to go. Heck, Jake Hunter probably built his own cell tower on the mountain.

Shaking her head, she hit speed dial and listened to the phone ring until her sister answered. "Hey, Claudia," Cassidy said, smiling. "Just wanted to let you know I got here safely."

Her younger sister laughed. "Yeah, Montana's not on the far side of the moon, so I figured you were okay when I didn't hear any news about a plane crash."

"Ouch." Cassidy plopped onto the edge of the bed and let her gaze wander around the bedroom she'd been given for the night.

As spectacular as the rest of the house, the room was as large as her entire studio apartment back in Boston. And furnished better, she added silently. Again, there were floor-to-ceiling windows offering that tremendous view of water surrounded by pines bending and twisting in the wind. There were colorful rugs strewn across the gleaming wood floor, a fire burning cheerfully in the hearth and two overstuffed chairs pulled up in front of it, looking cozy enough to be on a Christmas card. On a narrow table against the wall sat a crystal decanter of what was probably brandy, considering the two bulbous glasses beside it. But there were also two bottles of wine. Red and white and accompanying glasses—which she would so take advantage of as soon as she was off the phone.

The bed she sat on was huge and covered in a silky quilt in varying shades of green that made her think of the forest beyond the house. The mattress was so soft and welcoming, it practically *begged* to be napped on.

"So how did your test go this morning?"

"Aced it," Claudia retorted quickly and then laughed with glee. "I'm going to be the best damn doctor in the country by the time I'm done!"

"You will. And so humble, too," Cassidy said, smiling at her sister's enthusiasm. Since she was a child, Claudia had wanted to be a doctor, and now that she was taking premed at college, she was just unstoppable. Thanks to scholarships and the hefty salary Elise Hunter paid Cassidy, they wouldn't have to worry about college expenses and Claudia could pursue her longtime dream.

"So what's it like in the Wild West?"

Cassidy chuckled. "No stagecoach holdup if that's

what you mean. It really is gorgeous even though Elise's son is kind of…" Hmm. How to explain that rush of attraction combined with the troll attitude?

"Ooh," her sister said, "I sense intrigue. Cass is interested in an actual living, breathing *male."*

"I'm not interested." Okay, that was a lie, but she wouldn't admit to it. Besides, interest and attraction were two different things, right? Interest would imply that she was looking at Jake Hunter as more than simply a great-looking man with a crappy attitude. Attraction was an involuntary biological imperative for the survival of the species and—oh for heaven's sake, she sounded like one of Claudia's professors.

To her sister, she said, "I'm just here to get him to sign some papers and then first thing tomorrow I'm on a plane home again."

"Uh-huh. First thing tomorrow means you've still got all night tonight."

Yes, she did. Funny, but the thought of spending the night at the ranch hadn't bothered her at all until she'd gotten her first look at Jake. Now, it was different. That buzz of sensation she'd felt just shaking his hand left her feeling oddly off-balance and she didn't really enjoy that at all. Not that she would tell Claudia any of this, of course.

"Is there some reason my baby sister is trying to shove me at a man she's never even met?" Cassidy scooted off the edge of the bed and walked across the room to the window.

"Because my big sister has been living like a nun for way too long," Claudia countered. "You haven't been on a date in like forever. Do you even remember what *fun* is?"

Stung, Cassidy dropped onto the window seat, leaned against the cold glass and said, "I have fun all the time."

"Doing what?"

"I like my job—"

"Work is not fun."

"Fine. Well, I went to the movies just..." She had to think about that, and when she realized how long ago it had actually been, her scowl deepened. "Fun is overrated."

"Uh-huh." An all-too-familiar sigh of exaggerated patience sifted through the phone. "I'm all grown up now, Cass. You can stop throwing yourself on the altar of substitute motherhood."

Her gaze locked on that amazing view, Cassidy let her sister's words rocket around her mind for a second or two before she said, "Claud, I never thought of it like that."

"Oh sweetie, I know." Claudia sighed again. "Cass, you've been great. You've always been there for me but I'm grown now—"

"Yes," Cassidy interrupted wryly, "nineteen is practically aged."

"—and I'm in college," Claudia went on as if her sister hadn't said a word, "and you should really start concentrating on your own life."

"I have a life, thanks."

"You have work," Claudia corrected. "And you have me. And Dave. But our brother's married with kids of his own now."

True. It had been the three of them for so long, it was hard to realize that her younger brother and sister were grown and didn't need her hovering all the time as they used to. Especially Claudia. She had been only ten years old when their mother decided to follow her current "soul mate" into the sunset. So at nineteen, Cassidy had taken over. She'd been both mother and father—since their illustrious sperm donor parent had disappeared shortly after Claudia's birth—and if she had to say so herself, Cassidy had done a great job of parenting. Maybe that was why it was so hard to *stop*.

"Fine," she said. "I promise I'll find a life. Once I get home."

"Why wait? No time like the present to get started," Claudia argued. "You're on a ranch with a cowboy, for heaven's sake. That's a classic fantasy. Is he cute?"

Cute? No. Jake Hunter was way too manly to be classified as merely "cute." He was gorgeous. Or rugged. Or strong, masculine, gruff and all sorts of other really good words, but *cute* wasn't one of them.

"I didn't notice," she lied.

"Sure." Her sister laughed. "Anyway, my point is, relax a little. Enjoy yourself. Flirt. Consider it practice for when you get back home and I badger you into doing this for real."

Flirt? With Jake Hunter? Oh, Cassidy didn't think so. First of all, he was her boss's *son*. No way would she risk a great-paying job for a short-term fling— even if he were interested, which he probably wasn't, considering the way he'd talked to her so far. But more than that, Cass wasn't a one-night-stand kind of girl. She'd be uncomfortable and feeling all slutty so she wouldn't even enjoy herself anyway, so what would be the point?

God. Had Jake actually called her forthright? Her

mind was spinning like an out-of-control carnival ride. And suddenly, she was done thinking about this.

"Don't you have another test this afternoon?"

"See?" Claudia laughed. "You're way too focused on *my* life. Time to find your own, Cass! Love you!"

When her little sister hung up, Cassidy just stared down at her phone and thought about that brief yet involved conversation. Yes, maybe Claudia had a point, but in her own defense, Cass hadn't exactly been shown the most shining examples of relationships in her life.

Cass's father had abandoned the family when Claudia was born, saying only that three kids were just too many. Her mother had moved from man to man always looking for her "prince." But there were no princes, only frogs she continued to kiss in the hopes there would be a miraculous change.

So instead of following in her mother's footsteps, Cassidy worked, put herself through city college and made sure her siblings stayed in school. Eventually it had all paid off, of course. Dave was now a successful contractor with a wife and six-month-old twin boys. And Claudia was going to be the doctor she should be.

But, Cass thought as she shifted her gaze back to the view outside her window, maybe she *had* allowed work and worry to completely envelop her. And maybe Claudia was right that it was time Cass found out if there really was more to life than work.

Not that she would find that out *now,* she assured herself. "Good times do not start with a crabby cowboy no matter how gorgeous he is," she said out loud for emphasis. "Besides, as you told yourself earlier, he's your boss's *son.*"

Well, that should be enough to tamp down whatever lingering flickers of attraction were still burning inside her. She couldn't afford to risk her job by giving in to a momentary flash of heat that might or might not mean she was really attracted to the grumpy man downstairs. Not that her boss, Elise, had ever been that much of a tyrant or anything, but why take chances?

"Now that that's settled," she murmured, tossing her phone onto the deep green velvet window seat, "time to take a quick shower and maybe a little nap before I go downstairs and tend to business."

She walked to the bed, unzipped her suitcase and got out the things she'd need before stepping through a connecting door and coming to a dead stop. This house kept staggering her.

The bathroom was huge and opulent. Again, green was the main color here, but every possible shade of that color was represented in the tiles on the floor, the backsplash, the acre or so of granite countertops, the walk-in shower with six showerheads, and most spectacularly of all, in the gigantic Jacuzzi tub that was tucked beneath a bay window continuing the view of the lake and the wide sweep of sky outside.

There were lovely bottles and jars of soaps, lotions, shampoos and even, she thought with an inward sigh, bubble bath. Cassie had always loved lounging in a hot bath, but normally, who had the time? She glanced at that shower, then looked again at the tub that seemed to be calling to her. No reason her new acceptance of "fun" in her life couldn't start here.

"Okay," she whispered, picking up one of the thick white towels to lay on the wide ledge of the tub, "no shower for you, girl. Bath it is."

* * *

Jake tugged the collar of his jacket higher on his neck and tossed a wary glance at the darkening sky above him. A cold wind pushed at him, but he ignored that and strode toward the barn. Best thing to do was go about his business. Put Cassidy Moore out of his mind and focus on what was real. What was important.

And a woman who would be here on the ranch for less than twenty-four hours was *not* important.

The combined scents of hay and horses greeted him as he walked into the cavernous building. It was lined with stalls on either side, and some of the horses had their heads stuck out the doors, watching the cowboys at work, hoping for treats. Instantly, his mind shifted from thoughts of a very temporary woman to focus on the life he'd built for himself.

An hour of hard work, setting out feed and water and clearing stalls, made him feel better. Sure, he didn't have to do the dirty work himself, but concentrating on a task had always been the best way to soothe his mind. Of course, once the work was done his brain had too much free time.

"That's a pretty girl."

Rolling his eyes, Jake snorted. He didn't bother to turn and look at his grandfather. "She's not a girl, Pop. She's a woman."

"So you *did* notice."

You could say that. Slanting the older man a hard look, he said, "Yeah. Hard not to, what with her stumbling around on those high heels of hers."

"If that's all you noticed," Ben said, "then I worry about you, boy."

Jamming his hat down onto his head, Jake headed

outside. "No need to worry then. I'm not blind." He glanced back over his shoulder. "I'm also not interested."

All right, that wasn't entirely true. His body was *more* than interested. It was just his mind that was keeping things rational here. He'd been down this road before. Letting his desire for a pretty woman blind him to reality. And even as he thought that, he realized there was no point. The woman in question would be leaving in the morning and with any luck, he wouldn't see her again.

"Let it go, Pop." Jake kept walking, sure without looking that his grandfather was right behind him. "She works for Mom and she's not staying. Two very good reasons for you to keep your imagination in check."

"Pretty woman shows up on your mountain and you want to ignore her." A snort of derision followed that statement. "Youth really is wasted on the young."

At that, Jake stopped and looked back at the older man. "I'm not that young."

He didn't feel young, anyway. At thirty-four, he'd done too much, seen too much. After two tours of service in the Marines and surviving a marriage that never should have happened, hell, sometimes he felt as old as time.

Ben walked up to him and slapped one work-worn hand onto Jake's shoulder. "I know you've been through some rough times. But that's past, boy, and you've got to move on. The problem is, you're just too much inside your own head, Jake. Always have been. Spend a little less time thinking and a little *more* looking at pretty girls, might improve your attitude."

Jake laughed shortly. "My attitude's fine, Pop."

"Whatever you say, boy." Ben gave his shoulder another friendly slap then headed off toward his place. "All I'm telling you is that if I was you, I wouldn't be spending my time in the stable taking care of horses when I could be talking to that pretty girl."

Shifting his gaze to the main house, Jake thought briefly about the woman waiting inside for him. He was probably making more of this than there was. A buzz of sensation when he shook her hand didn't mean a damn thing. A flash of heat could dissipate as easily as it fired. This was simply a momentary blip. He'd reacted to her so strongly because he hadn't been down off the mountain in months. Enforced celibacy could make a man edgy. Hell, all he really needed was a woman. *Any* woman. That's why his mother's assistant had hit him as hard as she had.

Once she was gone, he'd head into town, find a woman and take care of his "distraction" problem.

Two hours later he was in his study when he heard Cassidy Moore heading downstairs. About time, he told himself and half wondered if she was always late for an appointment or if she wasn't looking forward to this meeting any more than he was. He could leave her to wander the house looking for him, he supposed. But then that felt a little too cowardly. So he stood up, walked to the doorway and looked down the hall.

One glance at her was all it took to reignite the buzz of interest his body seemed to be focusing on. She had changed clothes after her shower. Gone were the slick black slacks and killer red jacket. Instead, she wore jeans that looked faded and comfortable along with a dark blue button-down shirt and a pair of tennis shoes.

Her dark blond hair was soft and loose, hanging over her shoulders in thick waves. He watched her as she let her gaze slide across her surroundings and he smiled to himself at the appreciative gleam in those fog-gray eyes of hers.

"No more high heels?" he asked and his deep voice seemed to reverberate in the empty stillness.

She snapped her head around, her gaze locking onto his. "You startled me."

"Sorry." Though he wasn't. He'd enjoyed having a good long look at her without her being aware of his presence.

"It's okay." She brushed his apology aside with the wave of one hand. Glancing down at her outfit, she shrugged and added, "As for the heels, I just couldn't put them back on. First impression is over anyway, so I went for comfort."

"First impressions are that important?"

"Of course." She started walking toward him. "I represent your mother and Hunter Media, and even though you're her son, I have to be professional."

"I didn't realize my mother was such a tyrant," he said, amused.

"Oh, she's *not*," Cassidy said quickly. "That's not what I meant at all. I just take my job seriously and—"

"Relax." He interrupted her because he could see from the frantic gleam in her eye that she was probably worried about what he might say to his mother about her. "I was kidding."

"Oh." She took a breath and blew it out. "Okay. That's good. I really like my job."

"I'm sure. So. You have papers for me to sign?"

"I do." She held up one hand to show him the manila

envelope she'd brought downstairs with her. "Sorry I'm later than I thought I would be. But I lay down on that wonderful bed and fell asleep. Guess I was more tired than I thought. But I've got everything right here. Your mother said that she'd sent a copy to your lawyer to have him look them over."

"Yeah." Not that he was worried about his mother trying to cheat him. Although he wouldn't have put it past her to work in a clause somewhere that he would now have to visit Boston five or six times a year. "Everything's set so might as well get it done."

He walked back into his study and heard her footsteps on the floor as she followed.

Jake took a seat behind his desk and waited for her to sit down opposite him. When she did, she handed over the envelope and as he opened it to take the sheaf of papers out, she looked around the room, her gaze finally settling on the window behind him and the view so beautifully displayed.

"How do you get any work done?" she wondered absently. "If it were me, I'd be staring out that window all the time."

"One reason why it's behind me," he said as he flipped through the pages. Deliberately, he avoided looking at either the view *or* her.

"Sure, but you still know it's there."

He knew she was there, too, and that knowledge was far more distracting than even the sweeping view of the mountains that he loved. Jake picked up a pen and held on to it with a grip that should have been tight enough to shatter the steel barrel. What was it about this woman that was getting to him so completely and so quickly?

She stood up to move around the room, and Jake lifted his gaze just enough to see her. He zeroed in on her as she paused to examine the paintings hanging on the walls, the books in the bookcases and even the photographs on the mantel over the hearth where a fire burned against the chill of the day.

When she turned back to face him, his gaze dropped to the papers on his desk.

"This house is really amazing," she said. "You've got those same braces in here—the beams or whatever, that are made to look like tree trunks."

That had him smiling. Those support beams were a favorite of his. It had felt like bringing the forest inside the house, though the builder hadn't been thrilled with the extra work it had required.

Giving up on the illusion of examining the papers, he looked up at her and watched as she continued her inspection of his study. It was a big room, with plenty of heavy, dark brown leather furniture, and rugs in muted colors dotted the wood floors. Jake spent a lot of his time in here, so he'd wanted it to be comfortable.

"It's a big house for one man," she said softly.

"I like a lot of space."

"I can see that. But it would be a little creepy for me to have this big a house and be all by myself."

"Creepy how?" Intrigued in spite of himself, he leaned back in his chair and watched her.

She threw him a smile over her shoulder as she bent lower to inspect the books on the bookshelf. His gaze settled on the curve of her behind in that faded, worn, soft denim and a flash of heat shot through him with the swiftness of a lightning bolt.

"I'd always be expecting someone to break in," she said.

Frowning, he tore his gaze from her butt. "This isn't Boston."

"Oh, it's really not." She straightened, walked the perimeter of the room slowly and finally sat down opposite him again in one of two matching leather chairs. Resting her elbows on the arms of the chair, she folded her hands across her middle, tipped her head to one side and said, "Your mother really wants you back in Boston, you know."

"Yeah," he said, a reluctant smile curving his mouth. "She really hasn't kept that a big secret."

"She talks about you a lot. I think she misses you."

A ping of guilt stabbed at him, but he fought it down. Guilt didn't fix anything. Didn't change anything. Frowning now, Jake asked, "You're her personal assistant, right?"

"That's right. Why?"

"Aren't assistants supposed to be sworn to secrecy and discretion?"

She shrugged. "You're her son, and it's not like you don't already know everything I'm saying."

True. But he didn't enjoy having someone remind him that his mother missed him. He knew she did. But he saw her and his sister, Beth, and her family whenever they visited the ranch. That was enough. Jake wouldn't go back to the city again if he could help it. The closest he wanted to come to a city was downtown Kalispell, and that was only when he couldn't avoid it.

"So why are you so anti-Boston?" she asked quietly.

His gaze narrowed on her. "I know my mom didn't put you up to that question."

"No, that's just me. Being curious."

"Polite word for nosy."

"Guilty. You don't have to answer."

"Yeah," he said. "I know."

"But you will," she countered with an easy smile as she sat back more comfortably in the chair.

"What makes you think so?"

"Because you'll want to defend your position."

"Ah," he said, leaning back in his own chair. "But why would I care what you think of me?"

"Oh, you don't," she said. "But you can defend yourself to *you,* by explaining it to me."

Irritation warred with intrigue inside him. He'd known her only a few hours and she was already playing him. Were women *born* knowing how to maneuver a man into doing exactly what they wanted him to do?

"It's none of your business," he finally ground out.

"Ah." She nodded sagely. "The best defense is a good offense."

Surprised, he laughed. "You know football?"

She shrugged. "My younger brother played in high school and college. I went to a *lot* of games. And you changed the subject. Well done."

Shaking his head, Jake studied her for a long minute and found her gray gaze steady and filled with interest. "Okay. I grew up in the city. But this ranch always felt like home to me."

"And…"

"And, after college and the Corps, I couldn't settle in the city. Too much noise. Too many people. Too many things crowding in on me." He stood up, unable to stay behind the desk. Walking to the fire, he picked up a poker and stabbed at the smoldering logs until flames hissed and jumped to life again.

Funny, he hadn't thought about any of this for a long time, and remembering coming home from his last tour of duty and being surrounded by the crazed noises and crowds of the city brought it all back. That itchy, unsettled feeling that resulted in a cold, deep chill that had skimmed over his heart and soul, making him feel as if he were slowly freezing to death.

Grinding his teeth together, he swallowed hard, reminded himself that he'd left that old life behind and said, "I didn't belong there anymore. I needed space. Room to breathe. Couldn't find that in the city."

She was watching him. He didn't have to see it to feel her gaze on him. He knew she was wondering what the hell he was talking about. Considering him nuts for turning his back on Hunter Media and all that entailed. But he didn't face her; instead he simply stared into the flames and let himself be mesmerized.

Until she spoke and shattered the quiet.

"Really, I sympathize with your mother, but I can't see you living in Boston at all."

He lifted his head and shifted a look at her. He didn't see sympathy or concern or amusement on her features, and for that he was grateful. "Is that right? Why?"

She laughed a little and the sound was soft. "Well, first off, I do understand everything you just said. Sometimes the crowds downtown make me feel like I can't draw a breath."

He nodded.

"But secondly... Please. You wear boots and jeans

and a hat that you can pull down deliberately low enough to keep people from seeing your eyes."

A frown tugged at the corners of his mouth. Observant, wasn't she?

"I just can't see you sitting in on board meetings wearing a three-piece suit and sipping espresso."

He snorted at the idea. "Yeah, that was never going to happen."

"I think your mom gets that now," Cassidy said. "She's still disappointed, but she's accepted that you're never moving back to the city."

"Good. Took long enough," he mused. His mother had clung to the idea of Jake returning to the city to take his rightful place as the head of Hunter Media for far too long. It had been a bone of contention between them for years, even though he'd pointed out repeatedly that his younger sister Beth was right there, more than capable and *eager* for the job.

"But I'm curious."

His thoughts came to a dead stop as he looked at her. "*More* curiosity?"

"You never find out anything if you don't ask."

"Ask what?"

"Why the lonely cowboy on top of a mountain?" Her gray gaze locked on his, she watched him as if she could read his answer on his features. "You walked away from a dynasty in the city to come here. Why here? This mountain? This place?"

"Forthright again," he muttered.

"Not really. Nosy again."

He laughed shortly at the admission. "At least you're honest."

"I try to be."

Jake had once thought his ex was an honest woman, too. Turned out she was like most people. Honest only until it served her not to be. But what the hell, he'd give her an answer.

"When we were kids, Beth and I used to come here every summer to see our grandparents." His mind turned back, flipping through memories like a card-sharp about to deal a hand filled with images. "It was so different here. Bigger, of course. But more than that. Pop used to take me fishing and out with him when he was working the cattle. In Boston, I was a kid, told to watch out for cars, not to talk to strangers, and wasn't allowed to ride the damn T without an escort."

"Really? You couldn't ride public transit alone?"

He shrugged at that memory. "My parents were cautious. Always said that rich kids might get kidnapped. So Beth and I were watched constantly." Shaking his head, he continued. "Here, we were free. We ran wild all over the ranch with no one to hold us back. Went swimming in the lake, hiked all over the forest. It was a different world for both of us. But for me, it was the world I wanted." Grudgingly, he added, "When I got out of the Marines, I came straight here. I needed this place after that and—"

He stopped talking suddenly, surprised as hell that he'd told her all of that. Hell, he hadn't talked about his past in—well, ever. He didn't like looking back. He didn't believe in looking into the future, either. For Jake, the present was all that mattered. The here and now was all he could control, so that's where he put his focus.

"I can understand that," she said softly.

Jake straightened, set the poker in its stand and

walked back to sit behind the desk. Gathering up the papers, he began to read, skimming his gaze through the lawyer-speak with ease. He was a Hunter, after all, and he'd grown up knowing the ins and outs of deal making. "I didn't ask for your understanding," he muttered.

"Too bad," she told him. "You have it anyway."

He shot her a frown that she completely ignored.

"Just because you're a recluse doesn't mean you have to be crabby, too."

She made it sound like he was a damn hermit. He wasn't. He went into town. Just not lately. "Who says I'm a recluse?"

"Your sister."

Jake rolled his eyes. "Beth thinks five minutes of silence is some sort of torture."

Cassidy laughed and he found he liked the sound of it. "With her kids, I'm guessing she doesn't have to worry about silence most of the time."

He looked at her. "You sure seem to know a lot about my family."

"That's part of my job," she said with a shrug. "As your mother's assistant, I try to make her life easier—work and family. Luckily, I really enjoy your sister. And your mother is a brilliant woman. I'm learning a lot from her."

She jumped to her feet, came around the desk and leaned over his shoulder to point at something on the front page of the papers. "I almost forgot. Talking about your mother reminded me. She said you should be sure to read this clause especially well. Once you sign, it's irrevocable."

Jake tried to focus on what she was pointing to. Instead, though, the scent of her wrapped itself around him. Something cool and clean, like the forest after a rain. She smelled like springtime, and drawing it into his lungs made his brain fuzz out even as his body tightened. Damn, this wasn't going to work.

"Yeah. I see it. Thanks." He turned his head to look at her and found her mouth only a breath away from his. She met his gaze and looked away briefly before meeting his eyes again. Then she licked her lips nervously and the tightening inside Jake went into overdrive.

Blinking frantically, Cassidy moved back slightly and kept her voice brisk as she said, "Once you sign this, you're giving up any chance to come back and run Hunter Media. Basically, your signature is agreeing to accept Beth as the heir to the throne, so to speak."

"It's what I've wanted for years," he told her, grateful that she'd stepped far enough back that he could draw a breath without drowning in her scent.

"But it's permanent, so your mother wanted to make sure that you understood this can't be undone. She doesn't want Hunter Media's board to be unsettled."

"Permanent. Good." Jake nodded, and let his gaze drop to the sheaf of papers again. Much safer than staring into foggy eyes that held shadows and light and… damn it. He needed to keep his mind on business, but he wouldn't be able to do that right now. Not with her so close. "I'll sign these after dinner. Why don't we go see what my housekeeper left for us?"

Getting out of the study was a good idea. The kitchen was good. A huge room. Brightly lit. No cozy corners or any reason at all for Cassidy Moore to lean into him.

"Okay, I'm starved."

So was he.

But whatever they might find to eat, Jake didn't think it would ease the kind of hunger he was feeling.

Three

Dinner was good, if tense.

Just like the rest of the house, the kitchen was a room pulled right off the pages of some glossy magazine. Acres of pale wood cabinets, a heavy round pedestal table at one end of the long room, plum-colored walls and miles of black granite so shiny it glinted in the overhead lights. The appliances were stainless steel and the effect of it all was cozy and intimate in spite of its size.

The two of them sat at the table silently eating a hearty stew and crusty homemade bread left for them by Jake's housekeeper, Anna. Cass would have enjoyed the meal except for the fact that her host had pulled into himself and completely shut her out.

Amazing that only a few minutes ago they'd been chatting easily, and now, he'd become the recluse his sister called him. She had to wonder what had changed. What had suddenly made him close off to the point of ignoring that she was even in the room? Naturally, Cass couldn't take the silence for long.

"You *really* don't like having company, do you?" she asked.

His head came up and his eyes locked on hers. Cass felt the slam of that gaze punch into her with a kind of electric awareness that set off tiny ripples of anticipation over every square inch of her skin. Maybe she shouldn't have said anything. Maybe it would have been better to leave things as they were, with the silence humming between them. But it was too late now.

"What makes you say that?"

Cass shook her head and waved her spoon at him. "Please. You're sitting there like a statue—except for the glare you're shooting at me right now. You haven't said a word since we sat down to eat, and if body language is a real thing, at the moment, yours is saying *don't talk to me.*"

He frowned at her.

"See? My point exactly."

"Fine," he muttered, reaching for the glass of red wine in front of him. "I don't get a lot of company here."

"Not surprising since you're at the top of a mountain and the road to get here is a death-defying thrill ride," she noted with a little shudder as she remembered her drive.

That frown flickered across his face again. "There's nothing wrong with the road—"

"—that a few more feet on either side couldn't cure," she interrupted. "Anyway, now that you *do* have company, however short-lived, you could try to be...*nice*."

"Nice." He said the word as if he was speaking a foreign language.

Cass gave him a slow smile. "Would you like me to define that for you?"

"Thanks, I think I've got it." Though his tone was sarcastic, a twitch of his lips told her he might even be amused.

"Excellent." She took a sip of her wine. "So, let's try conversation. I'll start. This dinner is wonderful. Your housekeeper's a great cook."

"She is," he agreed.

"Two words. Not much, but it's a start," she said, enjoying the flash of irritation that shot across his eyes. "I know I keep saying this, but your house is just amazing. Every room I see makes it more so. But this kitchen, it's so big and there's only you to cook for. Seems a shame, somehow."

"Not to me." He pulled off a piece of bread from the slice in front of him and popped it into his mouth. "Besides, whatever Anna cooks here, she takes most of it back to her house for her and her husband. And then when there's something big going on, she cooks for the whole ranch."

Cass took a bite of her bread. "Something big?"

He shrugged. "Anything that keeps the ranch hands from getting back to their cabins to do for themselves. Could be a storm, or a fire on the mountain that we're helping to put out. Or even just a horse auction when we've got potential customers gathered. Cowboys have to eat and if you feed them well, they work harder."

Cass watched him as he spoke. For a recluse, he

could really get going when he wanted to. Of course, all it took was to ask him questions about the ranch he so obviously loved. Then his features were animated, there was a gleam in his eyes, and every word he spoke was flavored with enthusiasm.

She felt an inner sigh that she was grateful he couldn't hear or sense. Jake Hunter really was gorgeous. It wasn't fair that she could be so attracted to a man who should remain untouchable. Boss's son. Recluse. Geographically undesirable.

And yet…as she watched him, she felt a swirl of something hot begin to unfold deep inside her. His smile kicked her heart into an odd little lurch and the pit of her stomach felt as if there were a million or so butterflies lodged there. Not to mention the tingles of expectation that were settling in a little lower.

It had been a long time since she'd felt an instant attraction for a man, and she'd *never* felt one this strong.

And *why* did she keep hearing Claudia's voice whispering, *Go for it! Flirt! Live!* She couldn't do that, could she?

No. Absolutely not. Just thinking about doing what she was thinking about after knowing the man for only a few pitiful hours probably qualified her for Skank of the Century.

"Oh, God…"

"Are you okay?" He was looking at her.

"Yes, why? Did I say that out loud?" she asked.

"Yeah. So what's wrong? You feeling all right?"

"Fine, fine." Astonishing how much easier she was finding it to lie. Maybe she should be worried about that. "I was, um, thinking about the paperwork and making a mental note not to forget to get you to sign it."

Oh, that didn't sound pathetic at all.

"Okay, let's go get that done right now then," he said and carried his dirty dishes to the sink. He rinsed them out, then took hers and rinsed those as well.

"I like a man who cleans up after himself."

"Yeah, well, we didn't have a lot of maids in the Marines," he said wryly.

He turned off the kitchen light and darkness swallowed the room as they left it behind. Cass hadn't even been aware of how much time had passed, but apparently, it got dark early up in the mountains. She shivered a little as they walked down the hall and the world beyond the window glass looked black as pitch. There were no outside lights on, so it was impossible to see anything but their reflections in the glass as they walked.

Looking away from the dark, she shifted her gaze to the man striding down the hall in front of her. His boot heels clacked hard against the wood floor, and her own sneakers whispered accompaniment. Her gaze swept him up and down, from his hair, curling over the collar of his white long-sleeved shirt, down to the tight way his jeans clung to his behind. The man had a great butt.

Oh boy. Another rush of heat swamped her and Cass was forced to shake her head in an effort to dislodge the thoughts that came rushing to the surface of her mind. Desperate for conversation, she asked, "How long were you in the Marines?"

He glanced over his shoulder at her. "Four years."

"Do you miss it?"

"Sometimes," he admitted, and looked surprised at his own statement. "Things were *clear* in the military in a way they can't always be in the civilian world."

"I guess I can see that," she said, pleased to have something to focus on besides how good the man looked in a pair of jeans. "But I don't think I'd be very good at following orders."

He turned into the study, sparing her another look over his shoulder. "Odd, because my mother's always been great at issuing orders."

"True," she admitted, walking behind him to the desk on the far wall. The lights were on in the study, so the outside world remained just a mirror image of the inside, with darkness outlining the two people framed in the glass. "But she also listens to suggestions, and I'm guessing superior officers in the military aren't real big on that."

He laughed and nodded. "You'd be right."

But she could see him as a marine. Tall, handsome, probably gorgeous in his uniform. And there was the attitude, too. Sure of himself, confident in a way that most men simply weren't. Jake was the kind of man women daydreamed over, and if she wasn't careful she was going to fall into that trap easily.

Sliding into his desk chair, he skimmed the papers again and though it looked fast, Cass knew it was also thorough. Plus, his lawyer had already gone over them, so when he scrawled his name across the signature line in a wide, generous hand, it was almost anticlimactic.

"Done," he said and sounded satisfied.

"I hope you don't regret it someday," she said when he handed the papers over to her. It really wasn't any of her business, but he was signing over his heritage.

Any interest he might have had in Hunter Media was now gone and she hoped he'd considered this from every angle.

"I won't. This has been a long time coming."

Cass knew he meant that, but a part of her simply didn't understand it. He was severing ties to his family. Okay, not emotional ties, financial ones. But they were still *ties*. Family was something Cass never took for granted because she'd fought so hard to hold on to the pieces of her family that she had left. She couldn't imagine a time ever coming when she would want space from Claudia or Dave. She had spent years holding tight to the threads that kept her and her brother and sister together, and the fact that Jake could so easily walk away from even one part of his family mystified her.

"Your mother is hurt by this, you know."

His features tightened and Cass thought she had probably stepped over a line. But there was no going back now that the words had been said.

"That forthright business can be annoying."

"I know, but that doesn't change the truth."

"She'll get over it," he said simply and stood up.

His physical presence was so overwhelming, she almost took an instinctive step backward. Instead though, she stayed just as she was—though it cost her a jangle of nerves. "You're her son and you're turning down what she and your father worked to build."

He blew out a breath and looked down at her. His eyes were shadowed, his thick hair fell across his forehead, and she could see the shadow of stubble on his jaw with a clarity that made her want to know if it felt as rough as it looked. Then her brain took that thought and ran with it, providing her with images of that stubble rubbing against her skin as he moved down her body, lavishing her with kisses.

Whoops.

Instantly, she dialed back the hormone rush and tried to focus on what he was saying.

"My parents built the dream they wanted. I'm doing the same thing. My mother gets it—" he gave her a brief, wry smile "—even if she wants to pretend she doesn't. And if you're worried about Hunter Media, don't be. My sister Beth is the right person for the job of running the company."

"Maybe," she said and wondered why she was saying all of this. Elise hadn't asked Cass to intervene on her behalf and would probably be horrified if she knew that Cass was haranguing her son over a decision that had been made months ago. But Cass couldn't seem to stop herself from continuing. "But your mother hates that you're so far away. Hates that you don't want to be a part of their daily lives."

Frowning, he eased down until one hip rested on the edge of his desk and their eyes were leveled on each other. "Why are you trying so hard? What does any of this matter to you?"

"Because it's not about the business. Though," she added as an aside, "most people would kill to be a part of Hunter Media. It's about family, and for me, that's important."

Even in the shadows, she saw his features tighten again and she wondered if *she* was the only one who could irritate him so easily.

"And you think my family's not important to me."

"I didn't *say* that."

"Didn't have to." His blue eyes darkened. "I don't know why I'm even bothering to talk to you about this. You've only been here a few hours. You don't know me, yet you think you can tell me what my life and my family should mean to me."

Cass winced, knowing she had that coming.

"I'm going to say this flat out. Listen close because I won't be repeating it. I love my family. That doesn't mean I'm willing to live in a crowded, noisy city to prove it. This is my life. This ranch. This mountain. Loving them doesn't mean I'm willing to give up on my own dreams. And since I was a kid, my dreams were centered *here*."

His voice was rough and low, and carried a passion she had already noticed appeared only when he was talking about the home he'd built here. He was defending his choices to her when he really didn't owe her any explanation at all. And she wondered why he was telling her this rather than stalking out of the room.

"You're right," she said. "I don't know you and it's none of my business what you do. I was just—"

"Doesn't matter," he said and picked up the sheaf of papers from the top of his desk. Handing them over to her, he said, "It's done now."

Cass hated being interrupted, but it was clear that he was finished with this conversation and completely uninterested in any kind of apology she might make. His hand brushed hers as Cass took the papers and she felt that same zing of electricity that she'd experienced before. Worse, she was sure he felt it too, because his eyes narrowed and darkened—which told her he was no happier about it than she was.

The room seemed smaller all of a sudden. As if the

walls had shrunk to encapsulate the two of them in a space that now felt…intimate, somehow.

"I should probably head out to the barn," he said, voice hard and low. "Check on the horses."

"Right," she agreed. "And I should go upstairs. I have to leave early in the morning to catch my flight back to Boston."

"Yeah," he murmured, bending his head toward her. "Good idea."

"I can catch up on some work before going to bed," she whispered, though work had never been further from her mind. She could feel the heat of his body reaching out to her and she leaned in, tipping her head back to watch his face as he came closer and closer.

"That'd be best," he said, gaze moving over her face before coming back to her eyes.

He didn't have to say a word for her to know what he was thinking—mainly because she was thinking the same thing. Lust was alive and well and eagerly jumping up and down in the corner of the room. An electrical field seemed to be snapping and sizzling between them, heightening every breath, every feeling, every desire.

"This would be a really bad idea," Cass said, licking her lips in anticipation of the kiss she knew was a breath away.

"No doubt," he agreed and took her mouth with his.

Heat exploded inside her. Cass's brain shut down with a nearly audible thud as her body, her wants and needs, took over. She dropped the signed papers and reached up to encircle his neck. He pulled her in close, his arms firm bands around her midsection as he held her in place, pressed tightly to him.

Her mouth opened under his and the first swipe of his tongue stole what was left of her breath. She groaned a little as she gave herself up to the amazing response quickening inside her. Cass had been kissed before, of course, but nothing she'd ever experienced could have prepared her for what she felt now.

It was as if she were lit up from the inside. Sparks of reaction sizzled in her bloodstream, and her heartbeat was loud enough to be deafening. Her stomach pitched and swirled and a heavy, throbbing ache began at the core of her. Need clawed at the base of her throat and she went with it.

Threading her fingers through his thick, soft hair, she held his head to hers and responded to his kiss with everything she had. Their tongues tangled together in a dance of passion that could lead to only one place. One place she suddenly wanted to go more than anything.

It didn't matter that she hardly knew him. Didn't matter that she would only be in his house one night. Didn't matter that she could hear "Skank Alarms" ringing distantly in her mind. All that *did* matter was the next moment. The next touch.

His hands swept up and down her back while his mouth plundered hers hungrily. She felt his touch as bolts of heat driven down into her bones, and still she wanted more. There was a desperation between them. A raw, pulsing need that clamored to be answered.

When he shifted his hold on her and covered one of her breasts with his palm, Cass broke free of his kiss to gasp in renewed pleasure. His thumb stroked across her hardened nipple and even through the fabric of her shirt and her bra, the heat of his caress jolted her.

"This is a mistake," he whispered as he quickly undid the buttons lining the front of her shirt.

"Absolutely," she agreed, and turned so he wouldn't have to reach too far to get to his goal.

"We should definitely stop before this gets out of control."

She opened her eyes, stared into his and asked, "What's *control?*"

He laughed shortly. "Good point."

Then her shirt was opened, his hand was over the lacy cup of her bra, and her already hard nipple seemed to strain to punch its way through the delicate fabric just to reach him.

Cass moaned softly and shifted her gaze past him as she focused only on what he was making her feel. Making her *want.* That's when she became alert enough to notice and remember that there was a wall of windows right behind them and that if anyone happened by this side of the house they were going to get quite the show.

"Oh, God!" She jerked in his arms and turned her back to the glass.

"What is it?"

"Windows," she muttered. "The whole world's watching..."

He laughed and Cass scowled at him. "Not funny."

"Also not an issue," he told her, turning her back around to face him. "When the house was built I had all of the glass treated. We can see out but no one can see in."

Relief coursed through her as she looked up into his eyes. "Really?"

"Really." He stroked the tip of one finger down the

center of her chest and she shivered. "Remember me? The recluse? The guy who likes privacy?"

"Privacy's good…"

With the edges of her shirt still hanging open, it was easy for him to flick open the front clasp of her bra, baring her breasts to him. The kiss of the cool air on her skin gave her a chill, but the heat of his touch followed so quickly after, Cass hardly noticed.

Now that she knew no one could see them, there was almost a thrill to standing in front of those windows while he touched her. She could see their reflection in the glass and was mesmerized as his hands covered her breasts. His thumbs moved over her erect nipples, stroking, pulling, teasing, and everything in her lit up in reaction. Her heartbeat sped up, that throbbing ache between her thighs became more insistent, and her breath puffed in and out of her lungs in short, sharp gasps.

Then he bent his head and took one of her nipples into his mouth and what was left of the slippery threads of her control disappeared. All there was, was this moment. This man. His incredibly talented mouth.

Crazy or not, she was really going to do this. She was going to have sex with her boss's son and she wasn't going to regret it later, either. "Jake…"

"Yeah." He lifted his head only long enough to take her mouth again in a brief, hard kiss. "We should move this upstairs and—"

In the distance, the front door slammed and they both jolted.

"Jake?" A man's shout, echoing throughout the house.

"Damn it," Jake muttered, "that's my foreman, Charlie. Something must be wrong."

"Go," she whispered frantically, "go."

He did, stalking from the room and down the hall. His boot heels sounded fainter and fainter the farther away he got. Fingers shaking, head still a little buzzed from sensation overload, Cass quickly hooked her bra and then did up the buttons on her shirt. Running her hands through her hair, she took a breath and nearly groaned as reality came crashing down on her.

For those few wonderful, amazing stolen moments, she'd forgotten about everything but what it had felt like to be touched by Jake. But now the chill of the room was overtaking the residual heat inside her, and clarity was also rearing up its ugly head.

That skank alarm she'd heard so distantly was now clanging like church bells, reverberating through her brain. What had she been thinking? Well, that answer was easy enough. She hadn't been. Not at all. She'd given in to what she was feeling without a single thought for what would inevitably come after.

Now, with a few moments to actually have a thought and recognize it, she knew that what they'd almost done would have been a colossal mistake. She was here for *one night*. What if Elise found out? Her boss had sent her out here on business, not to jump into bed with her son. Oh God, this was just so humiliating.

Before she had time to really revel in what an idiot she was, Cass heard Jake coming back to the study. The man's boots pounded against the floor in obviously hurried strides. She couldn't be standing here waiting to be ravished when he arrived, either. Cass bent down, scooped up the signed papers from the floor and clutched them to her chest like a medieval shield.

She would have to let him down nicely. Tell him that she'd done some thinking—*finally*—and that it would be better if they both forgot about what had happened.

"That's it. Easy," she whispered and hoped when she talked to Jake she sounded more confident. Because even *she* didn't believe her.

He stopped in the open doorway and the shadows hid most of his expression. All she could really see was the grim slash of his mouth as he stared at her.

"Look," he said tightly. "I'm needed out in the barn, so I can't be in here with you."

Disappointment and regret bubbled up inside her in spite of the fact that she'd been about to give him nearly the same speech. He was cutting her off before she could do the same to him. Why that bothered her, she couldn't have said. "Is there a problem?"

He walked farther into the room and now she could see his eyes. They were flat and cool, and absolutely none of the passion she'd seen moments ago was visible now. He stood stiffly, shoulders squared, like the marine he had been. It was as if he'd already distanced himself from her and was now only going through the physical motions.

"Yeah," he said. "There is. One of the mares is in labor. Not going well. The vet's on her way here now."

Each word was bitten off as if he resented having to be here at all, explaining himself.

"Okay," she said, clutching the paperwork even more tightly to her. "That's probably best anyway."

"Probably," he agreed and turned for the door. Before he left, though, he took another long look at her over his shoulder. That's when Cass knew the heat they'd shared wasn't gone.

It was being ignored.

Jake was tired as hell and still wound so tight from tangling with Cass that he could hardly walk without wincing in pain. Hell, he hadn't been this hard and achy for a woman in longer than he cared to remember.

He'd had a lucky break last night, getting called away before he could give in to the desire that had been eating away at him for hours. The taste of her had haunted him all night. The images of her face, her body, swam through his mind like a movie on constant repeat. He remembered every touch and how her skin—silky, smooth—had felt beneath his calloused hands.

And he'd told himself, in spite of all of that, that it was a good thing they'd been interrupted. One-night stands were bad enough, but with his mother's personal assistant? That was asking for grief he didn't need. Besides, he'd already tried being involved with a woman who didn't understand his need to be here on the mountain. Damned if he'd go through that again.

He'd built the life he loved. Cass didn't have a place in it. No woman did. He'd never let another one get close—no matter how much he wanted her.

So the next few days were going to be uncomfortable, to say the least. Because his lucky break was over and he was about to get tossed into the flames.

He heard her coming downstairs and walked to the front of the house to meet her. She looked pretty in those sleek black slacks, a deep green shirt and that bright red blazer. She was even wearing her heels again. He had thought that seeing her in those city clothes, back in her professional assistant role, would ease some of the fire inside him. He was wrong.

She smiled and said, "I just came down for some coffee before I head to the airport."

"You're not going to the airport today," he told her.

"What?" Frowning, she came down the last few steps to stand beside him. "Of course I am. My flight leaves in two hours."

He took her hand, drew her to the front door and threw it wide. "It's going to leave without you, Cass. There's no way to get down the mountain."

She stared at the yard and he watched her eyes widen and her jaw drop. He knew how she felt, and the snow wasn't even a surprise to him. He'd still been in the barn dealing with the mare when the early storm rolled in. And in the hours since, the steel-gray clouds overhead had dropped at least eight inches of fresh snow and it was still falling.

A cold wind sighed into the house, wrapping itself around the two people standing in the doorway. The walkways hadn't been plowed yet, so the whole yard looked magical and untouched.

"It's only October," she murmured.

"Welcome to Montana," he said, giving her hand a squeeze before releasing her. "The roads to and from the ranch are closed. It'll be a few days before the plows get up this high, so you're not going anywhere."

"But—" She tore her gaze from the white world spilling out in front of her to look up at him.

He met her gaze and felt as if he were sealing his own fate as he said, "Looks like we're stuck with each other."

Four

"It's been two days," Ben said, "and you've spent most of that time as far away from that woman as possible."

Jake glared at his grandfather. "What's your point?"

Ben leaned one arm on the top board of the stall gate and got comfy. "My point is, whether you like it or not, this storm has stranded Cassidy here and you owe it to your guest to make her feel welcome."

Jake continued rubbing down his horse. They'd spent the last two hours riding through the heavy snow, checking on the small herd of prize cattle the Hunter ranch held. It was cold and wet and miserable and pretty much summed up Jake's mood. And still it was better than hanging around the ranch house, smelling Cassidy's presence in every room.

"She's not a guest," he argued. "She's trapped here."

"A reluctant guest is still a guest," Ben countered, then crossed his arms on the fence slat, propped his chin on his arms and asked, "What is it about her that has you hiding out?"

That statement brought a snort of derision. "I don't *hide*. I've got work to do. Don't have time to babysit a bored woman with nothing to do. Besides," he added, "I saw her last night. She was on her laptop doing some work for Mom on the internet. I figure that's what she's still doing. And she doesn't need my help with that."

Of course, he couldn't be sure what she was up to because Jake had left the house at dawn that morning with most of the ranch hands. Hard enough trying to sleep just down the hall from her room; seeing her wasn't going to help the situation any. Besides, he had work to do. And if that work kept him away from Cassidy Moore, well, he considered that a bonus.

Normally, Jake didn't mind an early snowstorm closing off the mountain from visitors. Kept things quiet. But this storm was damned inconvenient.

"Think you've got her all figured out, do you?"

Jake slanted a hard look at his grandfather. When the hell had the older man become so damn nosy? But even as he thought it, Jake realized that Ben was always keeping his hand in what went on at the ranch—the difference now was, with Cassidy here, Ben had something beyond ranch business to be interested in.

Problem was, Jake was interested in her, too, though far differently from his grandfather. Not in a forever kind of way, though. He would never try that again. But he had a hell of a lot of interest in one night with Cassidy—whether it was a good idea or not. And it really was not a good idea.

"I do have her figured out." Jake ran the brush across his horse's back in long, even strokes that practically had the big animal purring. When he spoke again it wasn't just to his grandfather. He needed to hear it all said out loud, too.

"She's from the city, Pop. When it snows in Boston, there are snowplows out making the streets navigable. Sidewalks are swept off and my guess is she wouldn't know what to do with herself any more than Lisa did when the snow's up to your thigh and just walking across the yard is more aerobic exercise than most people get in a year."

"Always comes back to Lisa, doesn't it?"

Jake stopped brushing the horse and looked at his grandfather. "Why wouldn't it? She was my wife."

"*Was* being the operative word here."

Jake sighed. "You're the one who told me if you're going to make mistakes, don't make the same one over and over again. Remember?"

Scowling, Ben said, "I remember. But I don't see Lisa around here anywhere, so—"

"Maybe she's not here in person, but Lisa was as attached to her computer as Cassidy seems to be. They're both from the city. And I'm willing to bet that neither of them knows anything about ranch life or how to do anything more strenuous than hitting a keyboard without breaking a nail."

Shaking his head, Ben Hawkins blew out a breath and said, "You remind me of that old saying about the guy who got cheated by a Frenchman and then swore that *all* of the French were thieves."

"I didn't—"

"That's just stupid thinking if you ask me. You lump

all women together and you'll never notice when the right one shows up."

Jake stared at the other man for a long moment. "Where've you been, Pop? I'm not looking for the 'right' one. As far as I'm concerned that mythical woman doesn't exist." But, he added silently, Cassidy Moore would make a great "right now" woman. He gave his horse one last pat before easing out of the stall and latching the gate closed behind him. Brushing past his grandfather, he said, "If it'll make you happy I'll go to the house now and check on her. Okay?"

Ben smirked. "If you want to check on Cassidy, then you should come with me."

Frowning, Jake followed after his grandfather as the old man walked the length of the barn before pushing open one of the double doors. Holding it open with one hand, he used his free hand to signal Jake in a come-here motion. Still frowning, Jake looked out and couldn't believe what he was seeing.

There was Cass, wielding a snow shovel alongside Jim Hatton, clearing the sidewalks and porches of the cottages and bunkhouse. The two of them were laughing and talking, tossing shovels full of snow at each other and in general acting like they were the best of friends.

"She's shoveling?"

"Been at it for hours, too," Ben told him with a note of satisfaction in his voice. "You took most of the hands out with you, so that left Jim to do the clearing while I saw to the horses."

"Yeah..." No big deal. The ranch had an ATV with a snow blade attachment. All Jim had to do was drive the damn thing around the yard, clearing paths and around the barns. Nobody had asked him to clear sidewalks and porches, too. That could have waited.

"Cass came out, said she wanted to help." Ben grinned when Jake shot him a look. "She had Jim show her how to drive the ATV, then they took turns. After that, Cass went in to help Anna fix dinner for everyone and when she was finished, she came back out to help Jim clear the sidewalks and porches."

"Been busy around here."

"Yeah," Ben said wryly. "And I never did see her laptop today…"

"Funny. Real funny."

"She's a nice girl. Helpful. Seems to know how to enjoy herself, too." Ben paused. "Maybe she could teach you."

Jake didn't know about that, but there was plenty he'd like to teach her. He shifted his gaze back to her in time to see Cass slip on some ice and fall over into a drift of knee-high snow. Her laughter pealed out into the cold, still air and something inside Jake ignited. Then that heat became a blistering fire as he watched Jim reach one hand down to pull Cass up and then turn her around to brush the snow off her back and butt.

A rumble of disquiet rolled through Jake, though he couldn't have put a name to the feeling. It cost him, but he ignored Jim's presence and focused on Cassidy. She was wearing a jacket that was too big for her, and a borrowed knit snow hat in blazing orange that boasted a pom-pom on top of her head. Heavy leather gloves covered her hands, and her jeans were stuffed into knee-high boots. Her cheeks were red from the cold; her hair, dusted with snow, hung down around her shoulders, and even at a distance he saw the joy on her face and knew her smoke-gray eyes would be sparkling.

She was having fun.

Working.

Outside.

Hell, Lisa had never left the confines of the house until all snow had been brushed aside for her. She had never taken the time to get to know the men who worked on the ranch, either—let alone work alongside them. All right, maybe Jake had judged Cassidy too harshly. But wasn't that the safest way to handle her? Knowing how she made his body react, keeping her at arm's length seemed the wisest decision.

"Not much like Lisa at all if you ask me," Ben mused.

Jake slanted his grandfather an impatient glance. Hearing his own thoughts voiced aloud wasn't helping. "Nobody asked you."

Ben only chuckled, which had Jake gritting his teeth. A hell of a thing, for a man to be thirty-four years old and still have his grandfather see through him so easily. He turned his back on the view of Cass and headed back into the barn. "How's the new foal doing?"

Another snort of laughter. "Nice change of subject."

"You know as well as I do we've got to watch a late foal—winter's a hard time for a horse that young."

"We'll get her through." Ben rubbed one hand across the back of his neck. "She's got a warm stall, plenty of feed and her mama to keep her safe."

"Think I'll take a look at her just the same."

"Thought you might."

Jake stopped dead and looked over his shoulder at

his grandfather. "This has nothing to do with avoiding Cassidy. This is about work. Responsibility."

"Real handy then that it also gives you a reason to stay put rather than face that laughing woman out there."

Jake scowled but didn't bother answering, mostly because he couldn't argue with truth. So instead, he walked along the length of the barn. Most of the stalls were empty as the cowboys hadn't come down off the mountain yet. But there were a few horses tucked away from the winter storm.

He took the time to stop and check all of them, starting with the stallion that was his prize stud. People paid big money to have their mares impregnated by Blackthorn. The big horse huffed out a breath in welcome, then nosed at Jake's pockets, looking for treats. "I've got nothing for you right now, but I'll be back with an apple later, all right?"

Jake would swear that the horse understood him when he talked, and the stallion gave him a disappointed shove with his big head as if to underscore that. "Okay," Jake said, laughing a little. "Two apples."

He locked the stall behind him and walked on, stopping to check on a mare with a strained foreleg. She was healing well, but Jake wanted to see it for himself. The horse continued to eat as he pulled up a stool, plunked down on it and began to unwrap the binding around her leg. This was what he needed to do. Focus his thoughts, his energies, on the animals who needed him. On the ranch that had become his world.

"Looks like your days of relaxation and pampering are about over," he told the horse and smiled to himself when the animal whickered gently as if arguing with him.

"You've got it easy, don't you?" he asked, comfortable with talking to the horse. It was a good time to gather his thoughts, to ease his mind. Talking to animals who couldn't answer back was better than therapy. He should know. He'd had plenty of that when he got back from his last tour of duty.

It was the nightmares that had gotten him a one-way ticket to a shrink's couch. Memories that he couldn't or wouldn't deal with when awake managed to slip into his dreams and drive him mad, as if he were still in a battle for his life. Images, sounds, smells, chased him in his dreams, hurtling him from sleep with a jolt, night after night.

But the therapist and all of her *face your fear, remember and embrace what you lost,* hadn't helped a damn. How the hell could he be expected to embrace a damn thing? What was lost was gone forever. What he had left was this place. *That's* what had saved him. Coming home. To the ranch that smoothed every rough edge on his soul until he was finally, he thought, nearly whole again.

And now his dreams were back to being haunted. Haunted not by the sights and sounds of war, but by a visceral need that had him wound so tight he could hardly walk without pain. There was probably something ironic in there somewhere but damned if he could see it.

The mare shifted impatiently as if telling him to get out of his own head and on to more important things. He couldn't agree more.

"Another day or two," he murmured as he ran his

palm up and down her foreleg. "Then you'll be good to go."

"Is she hurt?"

Jake's head snapped up to see Cassidy watching him from just outside the gate. Where'd a man have to go these days to get some time to himself? "What're you doing here?"

"I'm happy to see you, too." She smiled in spite of his less-than-warm welcome. "Your grandfather said if I came in here, you'd show me the baby horse."

"Foal," he corrected, then muttered more quietly, "Of course he did." Jake wished Ben would find a new hobby.

"So, is this horse all right?"

Concentrating on the task at hand, Jake checked again for swelling and smiled to himself when he couldn't find any. "It's just a muscle strain," he said, "and she's nearly back to normal."

Quickly, efficiently, he rewrapped the animal's leg, gave her a pat, then stepped out of the stall, forcing Cassidy to move out of the way. Good. Distance was key. And even with that thought, he caught a whiff of her scent, instinctively dragging it deep inside him. His gaze swept her up and down. His old jacket swamped her much smaller body and fell down nearly to her knees. She had snow dusting her hair, on that silly hat and caked on an old pair of Anna's boots, and she looked…happy. When his gaze settled on her face, he saw her cheeks were red from the cold, her gray eyes were dancing, and there was a half smile on her face. "You should go into the house. You're probably freezing."

"I'm cold but not frozen yet," she said, giving him another grin.

"Yeah. I saw you out there with Jim."

"I was helping," she said with a shrug, then winced and rolled her shoulders.

He gave her a knowing look. "You think your muscles ache now? Wait awhile."

"It was worth it," she said. "It felt good to get outside in the cold air."

"Can't argue with that," he said, walking past her toward the last couple of stalls. He understood the need to be outside, doing something, feeling the slap of the wind against your cheeks. He just wouldn't have thought that *she* would understand it.

The gelding he looked in on next had his head hanging out the stall door in anticipation of a good rub between his eyes. So Jake obliged while Cassidy walked up behind him and said, "Look at him. It's like he's a puppy getting a belly rub."

Jake had to smile. "Rocky always wants you to give him a pat or a scratch. If he could figure out how to do it, he'd be a lap-horse."

She laughed at the idea, and the sound of that laughter reached right inside to twist and tangle him into even more knots. The woman was dangerous.

"His name's Rocky?"

"Yeah, short for Rocking Chair."

"What kind of name is that?" She reached out to smooth her hand down the length of Rocky's nose and the horse moved into her, silently asking for more.

"He's lazy," Jake said with affection. "Even as a colt, he would rather walk than run and rather roll in a shady spot of grass than walk. So. Rocking Chair.

He's not a stud. No one wants the lazy gene passed on. And the only people who'd enjoy riding him are little kids for a slow walk around the corral."

Cass tipped her head to one side and looked at him, measuring. "Yet you keep him here."

Jake's gaze flashed to hers.

"The horses are your business and Rocky is, despite being a sweetie, not really a part of that business, but you keep him anyway."

Frowning, Jake muttered, "Who'd buy him?"

Cass only smiled and stayed right behind Jake. "Your grandfather says you have to take extra care with a horse born this close to winter."

"He would be right." He tossed a glance at her over his shoulder. "They're too young to withstand really cold temps, so we have to ensure they stay warm and well fed."

"Ben says you understand horses better than anyone he's ever seen."

"Sounds like my grandfather's talking your ear off." And apparently had plenty to say.

"I like him."

He looked at her, saw that she meant it and nodded in approval. Lisa and his grandfather had never gotten along. Not that it mattered any that Ben and Cass clearly did. "He likes you, too."

"That's nice to hear." She leaned on the stall door after he went through. "Oh, isn't she sweet?"

The foal was a charmer, all long legs and big eyes with flirty eyelashes. Still a little wobbly, the foal came close to the stall door and let Cass lean over to pet her head. The mare, of course, was keeping a close eye on everything, but Sadie was a good-natured animal and Jake wasn't worried. He went on, checking out the mare, giving her some extra attention, then made sure there was plenty of feed in the stall before slipping out the door again and latching it behind him.

Obviously reluctant to leave the tiny horse, still standing close enough to be petted, Cassidy spoke softly. "Your mother says the one thing she really misses about the ranch is the horses. I can see why."

He moved in closer than he should have, reached over the stall gate and grazed his palm across the foal's head. "Know a lot about horses, do you?"

She looked up at him with a grin. "Not a thing. But they're beautiful. And *big*. Except for this little guy—girl."

"They are beautiful," he agreed, and silently added, *so are you*. That smile of hers was deadly accurate. It lit up his insides like a fireworks explosion and he didn't need that. Didn't want that. So he forced himself to move away from her, from temptation. "They're a lot of work too, so I'd better get busy."

"Oh. Sure. Me, too. I guess I'll head back to the house."

"More internet work?"

"No. I promised Anna I'd help set out the meal and serve the hands when they got back, so I should get to the kitchen."

He frowned to himself as she started to walk away. She puzzled him. Intrigued him. Attracted him in a way no other woman ever had, and that was damned irritating. "You don't have to do this, you know."

She stopped and turned to face him. "Do what?"

He threw both hands out. "Help. Work. Cook with Anna. Shovel with Jim. It's not your job to do any of it."

Tipping her head to one side, she stared at him for a long moment. "This bothers you?"

"It confuses me," he admitted and could hardly believe he'd said it out loud.

She smiled at him and shook her head. "I don't know why. I'm here. There are things to be done— I'm helping do them. Simple."

"Why do I think there's nothing simple about you?" His gaze was locked on her. Snow fell behind her, twisting and dancing in the cold wind. Horses whickered softly in their stalls. Standing there in the coat and work boots and that silly hat, she looked as if she belonged. But he knew she didn't, despite appearances, and that stiffened his resolve even as she took the few steps back to stand directly in front of him.

"I think that may be the nicest thing anyone's ever said to me," she told him.

Then before he could think of a damn thing to say, she went up on her toes, reached for the back of his neck and pulled his head down to hers. She kissed him and he knew he should set her back, pull away from the tantalizing taste of her.

Just as he knew he wouldn't.

In an instant, he'd snatched her up close, pulling her into him until their bodies were pressed so tightly together, he could feel the heavy drum of her heart. She opened her mouth to him and Jake moved in, taking what he'd hungered for the last couple of days. Surrounded by her heat, her scent, her taste, he lost himself in the glory of it and shoved away all thoughts of caution.

Something raw and powerful rose up inside him and he rode the crest of that raging need, taking Cassidy with him. She moved in even closer, threading her arms around his neck and holding on as if he was the only stable point in her universe. He knew that feeling as the world around him rocked and swayed unsteadily.

In the back of his mind, a voice sounded, whispering, insisting that he stop now before he lost his grip on the last tattered remains of his self-control. And he fought the voice because he didn't want control. He wanted *this*. *Her*. He didn't know why she had hit him as hard as she had, but there was no denying the spark between them, the heat engulfing them.

The question was, did he surrender to the flames or snuff them out? Before he could make a call, the decision was made for him as shouts and conversation and bursts of laughter reached them from outside. His cowboys were back, headed to the barn.

Jake tore his mouth from hers and quickly pulled her arms from around his neck. She swayed a little and damned if he could blame her. But in a couple of quick seconds, she was steady again and he envied it. For him, the world was still slightly tilted and the pain in his groin was like a throbbing toothache.

"I should go. Help Anna."

"Yeah." He yanked off his hat, speared his fingers through his hair and sucked in a long, deep gulp of icy air. It didn't change a thing. "We'll all be inside soon."

Nodding, she backed up, her gaze locked on his. He couldn't look away either, because whether he wanted to admit it or not, he was done avoiding her. Done pretending that the need clamoring in his gut was going away. He needed her. Wanted her. And she wanted him back. Tonight, damn it, they'd have at each other and put the passion to rest.

She reached the door and had to squeeze past the cowboys and their horses. A few of them spoke to her, and she answered, but Jake hardly heard any of it. All he could think was, night couldn't come soon enough for him.

It was like a big, noisy family, Cass thought as she carried platter after platter of fried chicken, potatoes and corn to the table set up at one end of the massive kitchen. She was still amazed that the long table had folded out from the wall. It easily sat twenty, and could be folded down and tucked away when not in use. The house kept amazing her at every turn.

Of course, so did the man who had designed it all. Her gaze slid to where he sat at the head of the table, laughing at something his foreman and Anna's husband, Charlie, was saying. Cass's heart gave a little lurch in her chest. Jake Hunter scowling was enough to make a woman drool. Jake Hunter *smiling* made her want to climb right up all six feet four inches of him and settle in for a long visit.

Tingles of anticipation, flavored by memory, whipped through her bloodstream as she chatted and laughed with the cowboys. Anna had a good system here. Cook up a mountain of food and just keep it coming. The laughter, the good-natured teasing, the shouts, the bets on football games, it was…cozy, somehow. With the snow outside and the fire in the kitchen hearth snapping and crackling, this room was like sunlight.

Cass had always loved the idea of a big, boisterous family and now here she was, smack in the middle of one. She wondered if Jake even knew that his employees were his family. He was so determined to be alone, to have no connections, that he probably hadn't even realized that he was never really alone. Everyone here was important in his life.

And for right now anyway, Cass was a part of it all.

Her gaze landed on Jake again and he looked up, as if sensing her staring at him. His blue eyes darkened and a muscle in his jaw twitched. He was remembering their kiss in the barn. Remembering how they'd nearly set fire to each other with the heat between them. Heck, she hadn't been able to think of anything else for the last two hours. Several times, Anna had caught Cass daydreaming when she was supposed to be cooking and Cass didn't even have a good excuse to give.

"Cass, Anna says you made these chocolate cookies."

Shaken out of her thoughts, she turned to Lenny and nodded. "I did."

"Well that settles it, you'll have to marry me."

Everyone laughed, even Lenny's wife, sitting beside him.

"I'll run away with you as soon as Evelyn says you can go," Cass promised.

"Ready to toss me over for a cookie?" Evelyn gave her husband a slap on the shoulder.

"Really good cookies," he insisted and popped a piece of one into Evelyn's mouth.

She groaned, looked at Cass and said, "Forget Lenny, marry *me.*"

The people around this table were family. Mostly single men, who lived in the bunkhouses; only the ranch foreman, Charlie, and the head horse wrangler,

Lenny, lived in cabins with their wives. More laughter, more fun, and then Cass was looking into Jake's eyes again and the humor died away, burning in the flames she read there.

She wanted him bad, and if she didn't get off this mountain soon, she didn't know what she was going to do. Already, she'd kissed him. Twice. And sadly, she was forced to admit, only to herself of course, that if the cowboys hadn't returned to the ranch when they had—oh, better not to think about that.

The man had great hands. And an incredible mouth. Not to mention that truly fabulous butt. He was the whole package, plus fantasy bonus—a cowboy. Claudia was right, Cass told herself as she took a seat as far from Jake as she could manage, it had been way too long since Cass had had a man in her life. Those stolen moments with Jake told her it was time to change all of that. Oh, not now. Not Jake. Yes, she had kissed him first this time, but that had clearly been out of character. She couldn't do that again, and he would probably keep avoiding her until it was time for her to leave the ranch….

But when she got back to Boston, she'd look for a guy who could do to her what Jake was able to. Surely there had to be more than one man in the world who could send skyrockets flashing through her bloodstream.

Determined, she nodded at the thought, glad to have a plan. She picked up a piece of chicken, bit in and chewed, her gaze shifting unerringly to Jake again. He lifted his beer for a sip and she watched the muscles in his throat move. She licked her lips, sighed a little and told herself grimly that there was absolutely no man anywhere who could compare to Jake Hunter.

Finding a cowboy in Boston would be as easy as finding a stockbroker in Montana. No, when she went home, she'd be leaving the fantasy behind. The question was, would she go home with a smile on her face? Or regret in her heart?

Five

Once the work was done, what was she supposed to do?

Cass wandered the big, silent house and wished she could sleep. But that wasn't going to happen. She'd taken a hot bath to ease her sore muscles, tried to read a book and even flipped through a few dozen TV channels. Nothing had worked.

Now she was so unsettled, she couldn't even sit still. So she walked, her bare feet soundless on the wood floors. She paused to look at framed photos of the Montana countryside hanging on the walls. She ran her fingertips across the spines of leather-bound books on shelves. She stared out the windows at the dark night beyond the glass, then went on, moving into the great room, where a fire lay slowly dying in the hearth. The soft hiss and sizzle of flames looking for a meal on the charred wood was the only sound as she finally stopped her wandering and eased onto an overstuffed chaise covered in a blue-and-white flowered fabric that hinted of spring and promised comfort.

Taking a breath, she let it slide from her lungs and stared unseeing out the window. Her own reflection wavered in the glass, highlighted by the last of the firelight, and behind her lay the empty room. And then *he* was there.

As if conjured from the racing thoughts in her mind, Jake appeared out of the shadows and stood right behind her. His reflection joined hers and as he looked at their mirrored selves, he asked quietly, "Why're you sitting here in the dark?"

"There's firelight still," she said softly, gaze locked on the man in the glass. She could feel him behind her, and yet, the wavering figure in front of her had all of her attention. "Did I wake you?"

He shook his head. "Couldn't sleep."

She wondered why. Was he feeling what she was? The restlessness that seemed to nibble at her insides? When he closed his eyes, did he see *her?* Did he feel that kiss they'd shared in the stable? Did he remember that flash of anticipation, expectation, that had jolted between them?

Even now, her body was tingling, and staring into his eyes, dark in the glass, made her feel that tingle light up and sing. Cass had been over this and over this in her mind. She'd gone through the whole "boss's son" thing and she could admit, at least to herself, that she no longer cared. After all, it wasn't as if she would run home to Boston and announce that she'd had sex with Elise's son. No one had to know. This wasn't forever.

This was—she looked at him again and felt everything inside her turn over—*necessary.*

Silence stretched out between them, taut, humming with so much tension, it nearly burned the air.

"I like whatever it is you're thinking," he said.

"Not surprising, since I believe you're thinking the same thing." Her voice didn't sound the least bit breathy and desperate. Good for her.

He came around the edge of the chaise, held out one hand to her and, when she took it, pulled her to her feet. He didn't let go, but ran his thumb back and forth across her skin, sending shivers up and down her arms.

Cass looked up into his eyes and watched as they darkened, filled with the same need that she knew glittered in her own.

"I've been thinking it since the first time I saw you."

A swirl of something hot and lovely spun in her center and Cass took a long, deep breath, reveling in the sensation.

"Me, too." She couldn't believe she'd just admitted that to him. But then, not really a secret, was it? Each time they'd kissed, they'd set off so many internal explosions it had left her rattled for hours after.

"You should know—" He looked at her, hunger shining in his eyes, mouth tantalizingly close. "I didn't *want* to feel it."

She had to smile, how could she not? She'd been going through the same thing for days now. Good to know she hadn't been alone. "Now who's being forthright?"

"It's time, don't you think?" A small smile curved his mouth briefly as he pulled her closer. When he spoke again, though, all trace of amusement was gone from his features. His blue eyes were dark, serious and fixed on her as if she were the only person in the world. "I want you and I'm done waiting."

"Oh." She blew out a breath. "Okay. Good."

Time seemed to pause. Her mind raced with so many thoughts, and yet each one somehow allowed itself to be acknowledged before the next one rushed forward.

She liked him. A lot, really. Before she came to Montana, Jake's mother and sister had both told Cass about him. She'd listened to the stories and heard both their pride in and exasperation with him. She'd known before she came here that he kept his emotions on a short leash, that he didn't like company and that loyalty was important to him.

She'd heard about his short-lived marriage, his tours of duty and his love for this ranch. Once she got here, his grandfather had shared more stories until she felt as though she'd always known him. Yes, he was closed off and hard to know, but Cass had seen his gentleness with the horses. Seen him smile at his housekeeper and laugh with his grandfather. She remembered him with Rocky, the lazy horse.

Cass smiled to herself at the memory. He could tell himself that Rocky was only here under sufferance, because there was no way to get rid of the animal. But she knew the truth. She'd seen it in his eyes. He loved that horse and that's the only reason he kept him.

There was kindness beneath Jake's gruff exterior. And caring. And a capacity for love that he was denying himself. She had to wonder why. He intrigued her, attracted her and touched something deep inside her that had never before been awakened.

There was more to Jake Hunter than it appeared. And Cass wanted him so much the sensation was overwhelming. She'd never felt anything close to this need, this rush to touch and be touched before.

All of these thoughts and more swam through her mind. It seemed to take forever and yet she knew, logically, that only a handful of seconds passed.

Cass stared up at him and wondered how they'd come to this moment. Finding this…connection, with Jake Hunter wasn't something she'd expected. But now, it seemed inevitable that she step into the heat sliding from his body. That she keep her gaze locked on his as he spoke again.

"Good?" He smiled again and the way that curve of his lips lit up his eyes was simply staggering.

"Yes," she said, knowing exactly what she was saying yes to. She moved in eagerly as his arms locked around her and pulled her in.

"Glad to hear it," he whispered, then he bent his head to take her mouth.

That first brush of his lips against hers turned a key in a lock that was so deep inside her she hadn't even realized it was there. Every time he kissed her, she'd felt a buzz of rightness. A sense that it had been meant to happen. But this time, knowing that the kiss was leading to something more opened every door in her heart and mind.

She parted her lips for him and tangled her tongue with his. Breathing fast and hot, they gave and took and shared until her heartbeat thundered in her chest. She felt the same reaction in him as his arms tightened around her, holding her to him so that nothing separated them but the layers of fabric they wore.

And suddenly that was too much. He tore his mouth from hers, stared down into her eyes and said, "Upstairs. Now."

"Oh, yes."

He took her hand and led her from the room, and Cass was forced to run to keep up with his much longer strides. Her breathing was staggered, her pulse pounding, and when they hit the stairs, she was just a step behind him. Which was apparently too slow for Jake.

Stopping, he turned, swung her into his arms and took the rest of the oak staircase two steps at a time. "Wow. When you say now, you're not kidding."

He grinned down at her and Cass's heart tumbled in her chest. "No point in wasting time once the decision's made, is there?"

"No point at all." She hooked her arms around his neck and let herself enjoy being swept—literally—away. It was romantic, a gorgeous, muscular guy carrying her up a grand staircase to a bed that was—

"That is the biggest bed I've ever seen."

Jake gave her another smile and said, "Custom made. Big enough for me to stretch out."

"With a dozen of your closest friends," Cass whispered as he walked up to what had to be a king and a half mattress.

His room was as beautiful as the rest of the place, in a purely masculine fashion. Not that she had a lot of time to look around, but in a fast glance, she caught the dark red duvet on the mattress, and black leather chairs pulled up in front of a stone hearth where a fire burned brightly. The windows were bare, providing what would in daytime be a sweeping view of the ranch and the lake far below. There were bookcases, tables, and an adjoining door that probably led to the attached bath.

But most of her concentration was fixed on that bed. Especially when he laid her down onto the mattress and loomed over her.

"You're thinking," he accused warily. "Not changing your mind, are you?"

"Not a chance."

"Good to know," he said, lying down beside her and gathering her into his arms with a strength that sent chills racing along her spine.

His kiss woke every nerve ending in her body, leaving them all screaming for more. Her mouth opened under his and his kiss deepened until all she could think about was the next taste of him. This was what she had wanted. The mind-numbing passion that had eluded her for her entire life. Here, in his arms, she was thrown headfirst into a tumult of emotions and sensations that were too many, and coming too fast, to even identify them all.

And it didn't matter. Nothing mattered but having his hands on her. She felt him tug at her shirt and she moved to help him strip it off. The cool, slick feel of the duvet chilled her skin even as his touch heated her through. He tore his mouth from hers as if desperately in need of air, but then shifted to drag his mouth down the line of her throat, his lips and tongue leaving a line of fire in their wake.

She gasped and arched into him when his fingers undid the clasp at the front of her bra and spilled her breasts into his palms. At his first touch, she half lifted off the bed, moving into him as his fingers and thumbs tweaked and tugged at her nipples, pleasure darting through her at every action.

Her breath came in short, hard gasps when he took first one hardened nipple then the other into his mouth. His tongue did amazing things to her skin, his hot breath brushing her flesh with more heat than she thought she could bear.

"Beautiful," he whispered, his voice a tight groan in the firelit night. He lifted his head and looked at her. In his eyes, she read more passion than she had ever seen before. "Cassie, I want you badly enough that I can't promise to go slow."

Cassie. No one in her life called her Cassie and she liked it. It spoke of intimacy, a connection beyond the physical that only added to what she was feeling already. Hunger pumped through her. A need to lose herself in the feel of him.

"Who needs slow?" she answered softly and her words were swallowed by the cavernous room.

He grinned at her and her heart responded with that wild tumble again. What did he do to her? How did he do it? Days she'd known him and yet, to Cassidy, it felt as if somehow she'd *always* known him.

His hands were everywhere; she felt him. Every touch, every slice of heat that speared through her, driven by his caress. She moved and writhed on the bed, drowning in the feelings overtaking her. Too many, yet not nearly enough.

He dragged his mouth down the length of her body, stopping only when he came to the waistband of her jeans. Then his fingers quickly undid them and slid them down her legs and off. Her fingers fumbled with his clothes, too, and he let her have her way.

She skimmed her palms up and across his hard, muscled chest, loving how the hard planes of bronzed skin heated her hands.

Again and again, she touched him as if she couldn't get enough, and his response was immediate.

He jumped off the bed, practically growled, "Be right back," then stalked across the room to disappear through a doorway. Vaguely she heard a drawer open, then snap closed. Suddenly he was there again, before her body had time to cool at his absence.

Watching her, he stood by the side of the bed, stripping out of the rest of his clothes, then tearing open the condom he'd gone to the bathroom to get. He sheathed himself as she watched, her gaze locked on the hard length of him. He was as big there as he was everywhere else, and the anticipation inside her thrummed into overdrive.

"Been waiting days for this," he muttered, coming down on top of her as she parted her legs to draw him in. "Feels like years."

"It does," she agreed breathlessly. Oh, the heavy, solid feel of him covering her body was so right. So tantalizing. And then he slid inside her in one glorious thrust.

Cass gasped and moved with him as he took her over completely. He filled her to the point where she thought she would never feel empty again, with or without him in her life. She knew his imprint would remain long after this night was over—that thought squeezed her heart painfully, so she dismissed it and focused on what he was doing to her now. There would be time enough later for regrets, for pain.

He moved in her, his body sliding in and out in a

frenzied dance of need and passion. Her hands moved up and down his back, along his thighs, felt the power in his leanly muscled body and gloried in it. She lifted her legs to wrap them around his hips, pulling him in higher, deeper, and still it wasn't enough. It might never be enough.

Tension coiled inside her, tightening with his every thrust until she was gasping, lungs heaving for air that couldn't get past the knot lodged in her throat. And still she pushed him forward.

His whispered words, his kisses, all drove her toward the peak. She moved with him, around him, their flesh fused together by heat and passion. Cass groaned, called his name and reached for that dazzling light hanging in front of her. She had to have it. Had never known such bone-deep need, such desperation…

"Take it, Cassie. Take me," he whispered. "Let it go and grab for it."

"With you," she insisted, shaking her head against the duvet that now felt like a silky pool of fire beneath her. Shadows twisted, firelight danced in his eyes as she stared into their depths and gasped, "We go together."

He smiled, buried his face in the crook of her neck, and nibbled at her throat as he reached down between their bodies to flick his thumb across the hard swollen bud at her core. When she splintered in his arms, she heard him murmur, "You first."

Power slammed into her, shuddering through her body as she clung to him, soaring higher than she'd ever been before as he continued to move inside her, pushing her ever higher. The last of her climax was still rippling through her when she heard him groan her name. As his body rocked with completion, she held on to him, wondering how she was ever going to let him go.

What she'd just experienced would never happen with a different man. She knew it. It was Jake who had gotten past every one of her hesitations, her worries, and made her forget her reluctance to get involved with the one man she shouldn't.

And now she knew why she'd instinctively tried to hold herself back from him. It had nothing to do with worry over her boss or even the fact that she would be leaving and going back to Boston. No, this was more elemental than that. Somewhere, she had known that this man was the one who could reach her heart.

Jake Hunter was the one man in the world who could make her want to let go of old doubts and mistrusts.

To risk falling in love.

Jake rolled to one side and as he lay there beside her, Cass could practically *feel* him pulling away. She knew that right then, he was trying to find a way to let her down easy. To tell her that this didn't mean anything. That it had been a mistake and wouldn't be repeated.

But it *would* be repeated if she had anything to say about it. For the time she was in Montana, she wanted him with her, in her, over her. She wanted to wrap herself around him and luxuriate in the feeling of his skin along hers.

Because she knew, when she left, it would be over.

Oh, she hadn't counted on this. Hadn't expected to find…*him.* Now that she had, though, she also had to accept that she was going to lose him. Her heart pinged with an ache she realized would be with her for the rest of her life. But she hadn't asked for forever and he hadn't offered. Judging by the expression on his face and the shutters across his eyes, that offer wasn't about to be made, either.

So Cass would keep this light and never let him know that she was already more than halfway in love with him.

Turning her head to look at the man beside her, she noted his forearm tossed across his eyes, his chest moving with long, deep breaths and the *wall* he was already erecting between them.

As she watched him, he went up on one elbow and turned to look at her. She could read on his expression that he was about to start the whole this-was-a-mistake-and-I've-got-to-get-out-of-here speech. So she spoke fast, saying the first thing that came to mind. Something she'd wondered about since arriving at the ranch.

"Why don't you have a dog?"

His mouth snapped shut and he stared at her as if she were speaking Urdu. "What?"

"A dog." She stretched comfortably and smiled. "Cowboys. Dogs. They kind of go together, but you don't have one. I was wondering why."

Shaking his head a little, confusion shining in his eyes, he said, "That's what you want to talk about? *Now?*"

Cass forced a casual shrug she really wasn't feeling. "What would you rather talk about? How you're a loner and this was a mistake and how you don't want me to get my heart broken or anything—" She broke off and deepened her voice into an overly dramatic drawl. "I'm not the kind of man you need and you should just forget about all of this and realize that I'm not interested in forever?"

That confused look in his eyes was now tangled up with the first flares of irritation. She'd been right, of course. That's exactly what he had been about to say. Apparently having her say it for him didn't sit very well with Jake Hunter. Well, too bad.

Seconds passed in silence but for the log in the hearth that cracked in the heat and dropped to the grate below with a muffled crash.

"The 'talk' is unnecessary," she assured him, ignoring that tiny ache in her heart. "So why not ask about the dog situation?"

He huffed out a breath and frowned. "I don't know what to make of you."

"Forthright, remember?" Internally, she scoffed at that. If she were really forthright, she'd be telling him that she was almost in love with him and all it would take was a tiny push from him to complete the fall. But that would be like yelling "fire!" He'd be out of this room so fast, her hair would lift in the wind.

His gaze narrowed on her. "Right." Another second or two passed before he said, "I've got enough animals here that I have to care for. Don't really need a dog, so I've never gotten one."

She nodded. "I understand, but the horses and the cattle are business, aren't they? A dog would be more company than anything else."

"Who says I need company?" he challenged. "I've got twenty hands who work and live here—two of them with their wives—I've got my grandfather across the yard and plenty of clients who come and go. Not like I've got the time or the leisure to get lonely."

Though his words were firm and it was clear that he believed them, Cass thought she'd never met a lonelier person in her life. True, Jake was surrounded by all the people he'd just named, but he never let them in. According to his grandfather, even *he* had to fight to maintain any level of closeness, and she knew Jake loved the older man.

"Cassie," Jake said and the calm, patient tone of his voice caught her attention. "We really should talk about this."

Cass didn't want to. She didn't want to see him pull away, didn't want to hear words that had no meaning because she already knew there was no future here for her. So she rolled into him and slid one arm around his waist. "No," she said, looking up into his eyes. "We really don't. I'm a big girl, Jake. I'm in your bed because I want to be here. You don't owe me anything."

Emotions too varied to read darted across his face before he reached for her and pulled her in tightly enough so that Cass could feel his desire stirring to life again.

"You puzzle me," he admitted. "You never do or say what I expect you to."

Her heart tumbled in her chest at the heat in his eyes. "That's good," she said, brushing her mouth across his. "I would really hate to be predictable."

One corner of his mouth tipped up and he shook his head. "No worries there," he assured her.

"Jake, there's nothing we have to say to each other right now, okay?" She moved so that she could slide her fingers through his thick hair, each strand moving against her skin like a caress. "Let's just take tonight and not dissect it."

He seemed to think about it for a long minute. Then he said, "Storm's over, you know. The road out should be cleared in a day or two."

Another sharp stab of pain, regret, poked at her insides, but she ignored it. "Then in a day or two, I'll be gone and we can both go back to our lives. Good enough?"

His arm around her tightened, and for one heart-beat, Cass thought that he didn't like the idea of her leaving. She'd like to tell herself that he wanted her to stay. But the moment passed and she grimly reminded herself not to build illusions that would only shatter her later. Take what's here, she thought. Take it and treasure it, then let it go. It was the only way.

"I think we've talked enough," was all he said and then he dipped his head to take one pebbled nipple into his mouth.

Cass groaned and sighed all at once. Satisfaction and need curled together into a tangled knot until she didn't know which was the stronger. She held his head to her breast, sliding her fingers through his hair as his mouth tormented her with gentle torture designed to have her quivering into a puddle of goo.

Take it. Treasure it.
Then let it go.

A few hours later, Jake lay quietly in the dark with Cass curled up into his side. She slept, her breathing deep and even, her arm draped across his chest, her legs entwined with his.

His body was, for the moment, at peace. But his mind wouldn't shut off. The plain and simple truth was, he'd had his world rocked and he still wasn't sure how he'd allowed it to happen.

She was in his bed. Nestled up next to him. And he should be jumping to his feet and making tracks. Yet instead, he stayed here, next to her, feeling her breath brush across his chest. Inhaling the scent of her, drawing it deep inside him. He felt her heartbeat, soft against him, and felt invisible manacles snap closed around his wrists.

Well, *that* mental image got him moving.

Carefully, he eased out from under her. She whispered in her sleep, then curled up in the warmth his body had left behind on the sheets. In the moonlight drifting through the windows, he looked at her, that soft spill of dark blond hair, her creamy smooth skin, the rise and fall of her breasts beneath the quilt they'd been sharing. And the view shook him to his bones.

Deliberately, he turned his back on the bed and the woman in it and stalked to the adjoining bathroom. He hit the wall switch and winced as the lights jumped to life. Black and white tiles, black granite and black sinks gleamed in the harsh light, but when he looked in the mirror, Jake saw a man on the edge.

He curled his fingers around the end of that cold granite and leaned into the mirror. "What the hell?"

He'd wanted her for days and had assumed, naturally, that the minute he'd had Cass, the need for her would wane. It always had before. Every woman who'd come through his life—including his *ex-wife*—had left absolutely zero impression on him. If they were there, he was with them, but when they were gone, he didn't miss them. Hell, even when Lisa left him while he was still serving overseas, he'd been more pissed than hurt.

And when he'd come home, he'd easily gone on with his life without her.

Jake had always assumed that the lack was his. That there was just something missing within him that kept him from forming any kind of attachment to the women he encountered. But maybe, he thought now, it wasn't him. Maybe it was the women he'd chosen in the past.

Because he had new evidence. Cass was asleep in his bed.

And he wanted her all over again.

He turned from the mirror and the questions he saw in his own eyes. Walking into the shower, he turned the faucets and purposely stood beneath a fall of icy water. He didn't need more heat. Hell, he felt as if his blood were still boiling.

What he needed was cold. And distance. And some damn logic.

Lathering up the soap, he scrubbed his skin as if he could wash away her scent, but even as he tried, he had the feeling that he'd never be able to accomplish that. Cassidy Moore was a complication he hadn't figured on. He had to mitigate the danger to himself by getting her off his mountain and back to Boston as fast as he could manage it.

Just because he'd taken her into his bed for the night didn't mean that there was room in his life for her.

He was better off alone.

Six

Fourteen months later...

Cass's world was imploding and all she could do was stand there and watch it go.

But then ever since she left Montana, her life had been nothing but one shock after another, she told herself, so really...what was one more?

Leaving Jake had been harder than she would have thought. That last morning on the ranch, he'd kept his distance until it was time for her to leave. Then, he'd waved her off with a casual air—no kiss, no hint of regret to see her go—as if what they'd shared had meant nothing to him, and the pain of that memory traveled with her. And still, when she was first home in Boston, Cass had actually expected Jake to call her. To admit that he missed her. Naturally, he didn't. Stubborn man.

Then, two months after returning to Boston, Cass discovered that condoms weren't foolproof. She smiled at the memory of her shock and the thin thread of panic that had shot through her. Despite all of that, though, she had been thrilled to find out she was carrying Jake's baby. She'd always wanted a family of her own, and knowing that she would always have a piece of Jake with her had made missing him a little easier.

But the pregnancy had also meant she had to quit her job, because she couldn't continue working with Elise and not tell her about the baby—her grandchild.

Just as Cass couldn't tell Jake. Oh, her conscience had driven her nuts for weeks over that decision, but in the end, Cass knew it was for the best. Jake wanted to be alone and it was hard to be alone with a newborn in the house. And keeping her pregnancy from Elise wasn't easy, but if the woman knew the truth, she would tell her son and then…oh, it was a vicious circle. So in the end, Cass had kept her secrets, given up her job and built a life for herself and her child.

Sure it was scary, being a single mother, but it was worth it. Her son was her world and until today, she would have said that everything was going great.

Of course, that was before her brother and sister had shown themselves to be traitors.

Panic nibbled at her insides and every breath was a victory because it had made it past the knot lodged in her throat. Her heartbeat was loud and heavy in her ears and chills raced along her spine as she tried to come to grips with the worst-case scenario playing out in front of her eyes.

"I still can't believe you did this."

Cass needed to move. To get up and walk. Maybe

run. Problem was, there was nowhere to go. It was early December in Boston and even here, the snow was deep enough to make going for a walk less than pleasant.

So she settled for jumping up from the chair by her front window and stalking the three short steps to the opposite wall and back again. Pacing was less than helpful when the confines were so small.

Ordinarily she had no problem with her tiny one-bedroom apartment. But today, with her family gathered, she could feel those walls shrinking. While she stalked angrily, she sent Claudia another hard glare. "You had no right." Swinging her gaze to her brother, she added, "*Either* of you."

Claudia was unbowed and unrepentant. Her long blond hair was done in a single braid with strands of plastic holly berries woven through it. She wore a green and red sweater that read Santa Knows How to Deliver and her dark blue jeans were tucked into knee-high black boots. "Somebody had to," she said. "Dave and I talked about it and we decided—"

Cass turned her furious gaze on her younger brother. Dave's blond hair was cut short and he kept stabbing his fingers through it as if remembering when he was a teenager and wore it to his shoulders. His brown leather jacket was worn, his jeans and steel-toed work boots looked battered, and his features clearly said he wished he were anywhere but there.

"How do you two get to make a decision about *me?*"

He growled a little, shot a hard look at their youngest sister and then looked back to Cass. He followed her as she moved back to her chair and dropped into it.

"We *all* talked about it. Me, Emma and Claud, and we agreed this was the best way to handle it."

If she were any more furious Cassidy figured the top of her head might blow off and shoot right through the ceiling and the roof.

"You and your wife and our sister decided the best way to handle *me?* Since when have I needed to be 'handled'?"

"Since you started acting as stubborn as a sack of rocks," Claudia told her.

Another wave of rage swept through her and Cass had to fight to drag air into her lungs. "You had no right. Any of you. This is *my* life."

"Yeah, it is," Dave said and dropped to his haunches beside her. Looking up into her eyes, he said, "You spent a lot of years working to take care of me and Claud. We don't think it's fair that you have to do this by yourself. And more than not fair, Cass," Dave added quietly, his gaze locked with hers, "it's not right. He deserves to know."

He deserves to know.

Hadn't that sentence been repeating over and over again in her mind for the last year or more? Cass glanced across the room to where her infant son lay sleeping, completely oblivious to the family battle going on within feet of him.

Jake's son.

A child he knew nothing about.

Oh, she'd had an internal war over telling him or not ever since the pregnancy test read positive. She knew she should tell him, but at the same time, he'd made it more than clear that family wasn't important to him.

Besides, during their time together, they'd agreed that their situation was temporary. A baby wasn't temporary.

But it was more than that and she knew it. Though she had wanted to tell Jake about his son, she hadn't because she hadn't wanted to risk her baby's heart.

What if Jake got involved and then eventually pulled back? What if Luke was old enough to feel *his* father's rejection as brutally as she had felt her own dad's absence? No. She wouldn't do that to her child.

Although now, she might not have a choice.

"Why now?" she demanded, looking from one to the other of them in turn. "Why not six months ago? Or six months from now?"

"Because it's Christmas," Claud said in a huff. "It's past time he knew, Cass. And with the holidays and all…"

"Damn it Cass," Dave put in, "we're not going to feel guilty about this. You need the help and he needs to know he's a father."

"It was my decision," she argued. "Jake didn't want kids, so I didn't tell him."

"Yeah, that was before you got pregnant. It's easy enough to dismiss having children when it's theoretical. But when it's real, that's different." Dave's voice tightened. "He'd change his mind damn quick if he knew he had a son."

Her gaze shifted to him. "You don't know that."

"I'm a father. I *know.*"

"And even if he doesn't change his mind," Claudia added, "so what? The least he can do is help support Luke so it all doesn't fall on you."

Shaking her head, Cass said, "I don't want his money."

"Maybe not, but you need it," her stubborn sister countered. "Ever since you quit your job with Hunter Media, you've been scrambling."

"Claud's right," Dave said. "There's no need for you to kill yourself like this, Cass."

"You know darn well money's been tight whether you want to admit it or not," Claudia put in.

"I have plenty of clients," Cass argued, getting more defensive by the moment. Yes, she missed that healthy paycheck from Hunter Media, but she'd had to quit that job when she found out she was pregnant. How could she have kept on working for her son's grandmother and not *tell* the woman? But if she had told Elise, then Elise would have told her son and then Jake would have felt trapped into doing whatever the heck he considered the right thing and who needed any of that?

"Your clients are all great, but they're small-time and they don't pay you enough."

True, she was forced to admit—albeit silently, since she didn't want to give her siblings any more ammo to use against her. Her at-home billing business hadn't grown as quickly as she'd hoped, but it would.

"I can work from home on my laptop and that means I can be here with Luke. Whatever's missing from my old paycheck is saved by not needing day care."

"Uh-huh." Dave spoke again and Cass swung her gaze back to him. "But you'll need a bigger apartment soon and hopefully in a better neighborhood. That takes money, and there's no reason Jake can't help support his son."

God, she felt as if she were being attacked from all sides by the people who loved her best. She knew they were doing it because they cared, but what they'd done could change everything. Ruin everything.

"You don't get it." Cass stood up, unfolded the letter she had already read in disbelief a dozen times and shook it until the heavy paper rattled like dead leaves. "Claudia told Elise about Luke and now Elise is threatening to take him away from me."

Dave didn't bother reading the letter. He didn't have to. When Cass had called this emergency family meeting, she'd read the letter over the phone to both of her siblings.

"She can't do that."

"Of course she can," Cass snapped. "She's rich. I'm not. Luke is her grandson."

"She can but she won't," Claudia said, kicking back on the love seat and crossing her booted feet at the ankles.

It was extremely infuriating that her little sister looked neither contrite nor worried. "Oh really. And why not?"

"Because it would seriously piss off her son and she doesn't want to do that."

"I should take your word for it because you're such an expert on Elise Hunter?"

"No, you shouldn't take my word for it." Claudia sat straight up and met Cass's gaze with a fierce stare. "You should call Jake and tell him what his mother's up to."

Cass just blinked at her. As if she'd gone momentarily deaf, she shook her head to clear it and said, "Call Jake? I've been avoiding calling Jake since I found out I was pregnant."

"Which I didn't agree with," Dave put in.

Cass sneered at him, then faced her sister again. "I can't believe *you* haven't called Jake. You called his mother—betrayed your big sister and practically handed your nephew over. Traitors. You're both traitors."

Snorting, Claudia briefly inspected her fingernails, then pushed to her feet. "You've really become a drama queen since having a baby. I wanted to call Jake, believe me. And I would have, but I didn't have his number. I did call Elise because I figured *she'd* call Jake. I didn't think she'd make a play for Luke on her own."

Cass sighed and rubbed her forehead. Elise hadn't called her son. Cass knew that for a fact because if she had, Jake Hunter would no doubt be standing on her doorstep right now demanding answers. Why Elise hadn't told him was a mystery. But the meaning behind her letter was clear. She wanted her grandson and if Cass didn't find a way to fight her old boss, the woman would find a way to get custody of Luke.

Her pounding temper was turning into a pounding headache. Taking a breath, she focused inward, trying to find a solution to this jumbled-up mess her life had become.

What if she was wrong and Jake did want his son? Would he try to take Luke from her? Would she go to him for help only to find herself fighting two custody suits instead? And what if everything went great? What then? She'd been solely responsible for Luke from the start. What would it be like to suddenly have to share him?

There had been so many times over the course of her son's life that she had wished for Jake to be there with her. To be able to share the joyful moments along with the scary ones. And in spite of the worry shooting through her at the moment, a part of her yearned for the closeness with her son's father.

"Cass, we didn't mean to hurt you," Dave was saying.

"We were trying to help," Claudia added. "You've worked so hard your whole life. You took care of me single-handedly—practically raised Dave, too. It's not right that you have to do all the worrying and work alone again."

Cass sighed. "I know you meant well."

They loved her. They had been trying to help. Instead they'd created a tangled mess that Cass would have to solve. But she would solve it. This battle she couldn't afford to lose.

She walked across the room to stare down at her sleeping son. He had thick black hair and big blue eyes, just like his father. And like his daddy, Luke's smile melted her heart. Five months old and he was her entire world. Until he had come into her life, she'd had no idea you could love so deeply, so completely. She couldn't risk losing him. Which meant she really had only one option.

Jake.

This was going to be Luke's first Christmas and she'd wanted to make it special. Well, it didn't get much more special than meeting your father for the first time. Worry curled in the pit of her stomach. What would it be like to see Jake again? Her pulse skipped into a quick beat. So many times she had dreamed of being with him again. Now, it seemed, her wishes were about to be granted.

"Montana," she whispered, more to herself than her siblings, "here we come."

* * *

The last storm ended four days ago, but Jake knew there was another one coming in, fast. December in Montana meant snow. Lots of it. They were prepared as much as they could be, though. Generators at the house, barn and cabins were at the ready in case the power went out. There was enough firewood cut and stacked to last everyone a month and food storage was plentiful. They were ready for whatever Mother Nature tossed at them.

And still, he was restless.

"Probably Christmas getting to me," he muttered, standing at the kitchen counter staring out over the yard and the acres of white that seemed to fill the landscape. Every pine tree was draped in a solid cape of snow, and every oak and maple and aspen stood naked but for the lacy snow covering each of the bare branches and twigs.

He'd already made his traditional trip out to the forest to cut a Christmas tree for his grandfather, and then he'd had the traditional argument over why *he* didn't want one for the main house. Jake didn't do Christmas. Hadn't in years. In fact, the last holiday season he had "celebrated" had been on his first tour of duty in a war zone.

The guys in his company had built a "tree" out of whatever they could find—mostly discarded enemy weapons—and decorated it with string and bullets and paper "snow" torn out of padded envelopes sent from home. Missing their families, they'd all sung some carols, built a fire and pretended they were home. Until the enemy mortar fire exploded into camp, destroying the makeshift tree and killing two of Jake's friends.

He hadn't bothered celebrating since. For Jake, December was just a month to get through. Get past.

"Just as I'll get through this one."

"You say something?"

He turned to look at Anna as she hustled into the room and went straight to the stove where a huge pot of beef and barley soup was bubbling and sending out aromas designed to bring a hungry man to his knees.

"No," he said, pushing old memories aside to focus on the here and now.

"Fine then." She gave the pot a stir, then turned and braced both hands at her hips. Anna was in her fifties with graying blond hair, a thick waist and a no-nonsense attitude that Jake appreciated. "Charlie's back from town. He's just pulling into the front drive now."

"Good." Jake set his coffee cup down onto the counter. "I'll go meet him." His foreman had left the ranch in the four-wheel-drive Jeep more than an hour ago, without a word of explanation. And since Jake needed to talk to him about getting some hay out to the cattle before the next snow hit, he was anxious to find out what the hell had been important enough to drag him away from ranch business. He started across the room, then stopped. "Did he tell you why he went into town?"

Anna's eyebrows lifted as she gave him a cool, hard glare. "He did."

What was she mad about? "And?"

"*And,*" she repeated, tapping the toe of one boot against the floor, "you should go and see for yourself."

Anna was usually a reasonable woman, Jake thought, but at the moment, she looked angry enough to come at him with the spoon she still clutched in one hand.

Maybe Christmas was getting to everybody.

"Fine, I'm going." Shaking his head, he headed out of the kitchen and down the long hall toward the front of the house. Maybe Charlie knew what the hell was going on with his wife. Muttering darkly, Jake snatched his coat off the newel post at the foot of the stairs and shrugged into it. Then he tugged on his hat, grabbed the doorknob, yanked on it and almost plowed right into Cassie, standing on his front porch.

Her smoke-gray eyes shone with surprise, and her dark blond hair streamed down her shoulders from beneath a knit purple hat. She wore a heavy black coat and knee-high boots. Her cheeks were pink from the cold and as he adjusted to the shock of finding her on his front steps, he finally noticed what she was holding.

A baby.

Wrapped toe to neck in some kind of zip-up covering, all Jake could see of the child were big blue eyes— just like his own. A jolt of emotion shot through him so hard, he gripped the doorknob tight, to keep from falling over in shock.

"What the hell?"

"Jake," Cassie said, "meet your son. Luke."

Seven

"My *son?*" Silently, Jake congratulated himself on the self-control that kept his voice from raging with the fury erupting inside him. He looked into those soft gray eyes, read her defiance, and that damn near pushed him over the edge.

He couldn't believe this. For nearly a year and a half, this woman had haunted him, waking and sleeping. Hell, he'd hardly known her and shouldn't have given her another thought once she was gone. But he had. He'd missed her body and the soft, slick feel of her skin beneath his palms. The sound of her voice. Her laughter. The smoke-gray eyes that betrayed everything she was thinking, feeling. He'd missed the feel of her in his arms, the sighs as he entered her and the gasping groans when they each found their release.

Jake had even fantasized a couple times about seeing her here again.

He just had never imagined her carrying his child along with her.

His child.

He had a son.

She'd been keeping the truth from him for a year and a half and he *still* felt that rush of desire he hadn't found with anyone else. He looked at her and his body tightened, his heart banged against his rib cage, and his hands itched to touch her.

Didn't matter, it seemed, what she'd kept from him. He wanted her.

Grimly, he pushed those needs aside in favor of facing her down with the hard truth currently smiling up at him from a drooly face.

"What the hell, Cassie?" The words were ground from his throat as sharp and cold as pieces of broken glass.

"Don't swear in front of the baby," she muttered and pushed right past him into the house. Then she stopped, looking up at him. "We have to talk."

"Yeah," he said, torn between dumbfounded shock and pure fury. "I'd say so."

Anna came hurrying down the hall, glared at Jake and clucked her tongue at him so fast, it sounded like machine-gun fire. Then she dropped one arm around Cassie, enveloping her and the baby she carried, and steered them off to the great room.

"You come on in here and get warm by the fire," his turncoat housekeeper was saying. "And you give me a peek at that little darling, too…"

Jake shook his head and snatched off his hat, crumpling the brim in one tight fist. The wind rushing through the still-open front door sliced through his coat with icy knives, but he hardly felt it. Mind racing, emotions churning, his gaze landed on Charlie, standing in the yard staring at him.

"Sorry, boss. Cass called Ben from the airport and Ben sent me to fetch her."

Why the hell hadn't Ben said anything to Jake? Warned him? That was a thought for later. Right now, he looked at his foreman and said, "It's fine."

"I'll bring in the baby's car seat and Cass's bags," Charlie said, wincing a little at the words.

"Her bags? Of course she has bags." Seemed that she had plans to stay. Well, good, because she wasn't going anywhere until Jake had answers to all of the questions racing through his mind. Gritting his teeth, he said, "Take them up to the room she had last time she was here. After I talk to Cassie, I'll see you at the barn."

As soon as he could breathe again. As soon as he had some answers from the woman who had walked into the great room as if she belonged here. As if she hadn't been gone more than a year and given birth to his *son*.

Cassie had called Ben for help. And Ben had sent Charlie to the airport without a damn word to Jake. His own grandfather was a part of this. Then he had to wonder if Ben had known about the baby all along. Had he been a part of keeping Jake's child from him? Betrayal stung and fury roared fresh and new through his bloodstream. The anger churning inside nearly stole his breath.

Anna had known about Cassie flying in, because

Charlie had. How long had she known? Was she also in on the baby secret? She hadn't seemed surprised by it. How long had Ben known? Was his whole ranch in on this? Was everyone calling him a fool behind his back? Laughing at the man who was so clueless he had no idea he was a damn *father?*

Tossing his hat to the nearest table, he shrugged out of his jacket and dropped it onto a chair as he marched into the great room. Anna and Cassie were talking together, huddled around the baby, peeling his little snowsuit off while he jabbered and made nonsense noises. Jake stopped dead and watched the little boy from a distance.

His feet wanted to take him closer, but his mind was keeping him in place. Before he let himself be distracted by the child, he needed some answers from the boy's mother. As if the women could sense him watching them, they both turned around to face him. They'd stripped that cold weather covering off of the boy. Anna was holding the baby now and the infant—in a pair of tiny jeans, a flannel shirt and baby-size cowboy boots—gave Jake a grin that displayed four or five teeth.

Jake's heart fisted painfully in his chest. His throat closed up with emotions too thick and too many to name. A child. He could see the resemblance. Hell, there was no denying this boy was his son—even if Jake wanted to, which he didn't.

How was it possible to feel so much so quickly? Jake's instincts were kicking in with a force that shocked him. He suddenly knew that he would do anything to protect a child he hadn't known existed an hour ago. That boy was a part of him and no one would keep Jake from him. He'd already missed too much. Damned if he'd miss another minute. But for now, he needed some answers. Keeping his gaze fixed on the baby, he said quietly, "Anna, take him into the kitchen. Give him a cookie or something."

"You don't give a baby a cookie, Jake Hunter," she snapped. "But I think a banana would be welcome if that's all right with his mama."

"Oh, Luke loves bananas. Thank you, Anna," Cassie said, dropping a quick kiss on the baby's head.

His son loved bananas. *Good to know,* Jake told himself, still looking at the boy who had him hypnotized. His heart did another sharp squeeze in his chest as the kid laughed and clapped his tiny hands together.

Anna smiled at Cassie, then narrowed her eyes on Jake. "Anyway, I know how to take care of a baby without your advice, Jake Hunter," she grumbled and took the diaper bag from Cassie. "Don't you worry, honey, I raised four of my own. The boy will be fine with me. You come on in and have some tea once you're done with *him.*" She shot Jake a death glare as she swept past him, carrying his son.

Astonished, he looked after his supposedly loyal housekeeper for a long minute. This was nuts. Suddenly *he* was the bad guy here? How did that make sense?

"What the hell did I do?" he demanded of no one in particular. "I didn't know I had a kid, did I?"

Anna kept walking, her quick steps sounding like gunshots in the stillness. He turned away abruptly and his gaze swung to Cassie, standing there staring at him. Jake had the satisfaction of seeing her features tighten and her lips go bloodless.

"I know you want an explanation and I'll tell you whatever you want to know," she said in a rush, as she slid out of her heavy jacket to reveal a red sweater that reached to her thighs, and black jeans tucked into knee-high boots. She shoved the sleeves of her sweater up to her elbows.

Damn, she looked good. Having a baby had ripened her curves, made her even more desirable than she had been, and that was saying a lot.

Not the point.

"Start with why you called my grandfather to arrange a ride here from the airport. Why didn't you call me? Hell, while we're on it, why didn't you call me when you found out you were pregnant? When you had the baby?"

"I called Ben this morning because I didn't want to explain all of this to you over the phone." She pushed her hair back from her face and took a breath. "And I didn't want you to meet your son in the airport."

"That takes care of today," he ground out, crossing his arms over his chest. "Now explain the last fourteen months."

She took a breath and blew it out. "That'll take time. And there's something you have to know, first. The reason I'm here."

"You mean," he cut in, "the reason you're finally telling me about my *son.*"

"Yes." She reached into her bag, pulled a piece of paper out and crossed the room. Thrusting the page at him, she ordered, "Read that."

It only took a second or two and in that time, the temper he'd thought was as high as it could go burst past the breaking point. "My mother is going to sue you for custody of *my son?*"

Cass wrung her hands, tugging at her fingers, then started pacing back and forth across the huge room. While she walked, she threw glances at him. "My sister Claudia told your mom about Luke, and two days later, I got *that* in the mail. She'll do it, Jake. Elise Hunter will take my baby if you don't stop her."

"No one's going to take your baby from you," he muttered, gaze running over the few sharp and to-the-point sentences on the heavy stationery his mother preferred. "No judge would allow it."

"She's rich," Cass muttered. "I'm not. She can hire a fleet of lawyers and I can't." She stopped in front of him, tipped her head back and stared up into his eyes. "I won't lose my son. You have to do something."

Those fog-gray depths were filled with pain and worry, tugging at something inside him, awakening a protective streak he hadn't felt since he'd left the military. Back then, you watched your buddies' backs. You looked out for them all like family. Risked your own life to save theirs and never gave it another thought. Back home, he'd felt that same sense of loyalty to his grandfather, mother and sister—but with Cassie, that urge to defend came roaring through his blood like a battle cry.

Crumpling the paper in one hand, he walked to the phone on a side table near the couch. He grabbed the receiver out of its cradle, stabbed in a few numbers and waited for his mother to answer her private line. When she did, Jake didn't waste time on niceties.

"What's this bull about you trying to take Cassie's baby from her?"

"Well hello, Jake. So nice to hear from you. I'm very well, thanks for asking. And you?"

Cool, her voice had that dismissive tone he knew she used on business rivals. "I'm great," he ground out, gaze flashing to Cassie. "I just found out I'm a father and that my mother's trying to take my kid. How's your day going?"

Cassie's face flushed but her gray eyes were still clouded by worry.

"I won't have my grandson raised by a woman who can't afford to take care of him properly," his mother said tightly.

"He's my son and you're not taking him from his mother," Jake told her. "Hell, what made you think I'd allow that?"

"You've turned your back on your family, Jake," his mother said and he thought he heard a note of hurt coloring her words. "You cut me and your sister out of your life. How was I to know you'd feel differently about your son?"

"I didn't cut you out, mother. I cut the company out of my life. There's a difference."

"Not to me," she insisted. "You've locked yourself away on the mountain, Jake, and you worry me. You're so closed off, so self-contained, you don't need any of us. Well, that baby is a Hunter and if you won't do the right thing by him, then I will."

Furious now, his gaze firmly locked on the woman staring at him helplessly, he reminded his mother, "I wasn't given the chance to do the right thing. Nobody told me about that baby. Until five minutes ago I didn't know he existed."

"Well," his mother said softly, "now that you do know, what're you going to do about it?"

That was the question, wasn't it? He didn't have an answer. How the hell could he know what to do when the world as he'd known it had been upended in his face? Could he have five damn seconds to think?

"I'll let you know," he snapped and hung up. Tossing the phone onto the couch before he could smash the damn thing in his fist, he faced Cassie. "That's done. She won't be making a grab for the baby again."

"You don't know that," she whispered and he heard fear in her voice.

"I'll make sure of it."

A part of him wanted to go to her, pull her into his arms and hold her. Soothe her fears. Ease the worry shimmering around her like a stormy aura the color of her eyes. But a greater part of him was aching from betrayal.

From the fact that this woman had kept his son from him. Had kept his son's existence a secret.

"You should have told me."

She paled. "Maybe."

"Maybe?" He stalked toward her and inwardly cringed when he saw her dart backward a couple of steps. He wasn't trying to scare her, for God's sake. He only wanted answers. Explanations. But maybe he was too furious right now to hear them. Stopping in his tracks, he snorted a harsh laugh. "You really think I'd hurt you?"

"No, of course not." She shook her head and once again shoved both hands through her hair. It had grown, hanging down now to the middle of her back. With her jerky movements, long ropes of that dark blond silk fell over her shoulders to lay against her breasts. Rubbing her fingertips across her forehead, she murmured, "It's just been a long day. Luke didn't like the airplane ride. The passengers didn't like a crying baby. Then they couldn't find my luggage and the ride up the mountain road was terrifying and I just feel like…"

The tightness in his chest eased a little watching her. She'd had as rough a day as he was having. "Nice day, huh?"

Her head whipped up, her gaze locked on his, and whatever she saw there had her shoulders relaxing and a glint of humor sparking her eyes. "I've had better."

"Me, too." He still wanted to know. *Needed* to know. Everything. But there were things he had to do and he had to have some time to think. "Come on. I'll walk you to the kitchen."

Surprised, she asked, "We're not going to talk?"

"Later. Storm coming. Have to get the animals ready for it."

A strangled laugh slipped from her. "And we're back to cowboy-speak. That hasn't changed, anyway."

"Plenty else has," he said just as shortly, stopping only long enough to grab his hat and jacket. "And I'm gonna want to hear it all."

In the kitchen, Anna was seated at the table, holding the baby on her lap. On the floor, a big yellow Lab sat beside her, his nose on the baby's legs. The dog winced every time the baby patted his head, but otherwise, didn't move.

"A dog?" Cassie said. "You got a dog?"

The Lab pushed to his feet and came across the room to welcome Cassie with a snuffle and a few dozen licks. While Cassie heaped praise on the dog, scrubbing his ears, Jake could only think how much he wanted her hands on *him*.

"When did you get a dog?" she was asking.

Before he could answer, Anna did. "He got him right after you left the last time. Hardly a week before we had a puppy running around the house."

Jake glared at his housekeeper, but she paid him no mind at all.

He'd once told Cassie he didn't have a dog because he had enough animals to care for. But the truth was, after she left a year and a half ago, the damn house had been too quiet. Too…empty.

So he bought a dog for company. What was the big deal?

The baby shouted a babbled greeting and lifted his arms for his mother. Jake scowled, tugged his hat on and buttoned his jacket as he headed for the back door. "Come on, Boston. Work."

"Boston?" Cassie echoed the dog's name and Jake flinched as embarrassment swept through him.

Grinding his teeth, he managed, "I'm from Boston, too." When she didn't say anything to that, he added, "We'll talk later." He waited for the dog to join him, then opened the door to the blowing wind and snow.

There were heavy ropes strung between the back door of the house all the way across the yard to the barn. Ropes also hung between cabins and between the main house and his grandfather's place. When the predicted blizzard hit, the wind-driven snow would be so thick, flying so fast, a person could get lost between the house and the outbuildings. Without that rope to cling to, you could wander off track and freeze to death before anyone had a chance to find you.

But for now, the wind was light and the only snow blowing was lifting off the drifts and mounds already on the frozen ground. Jake hunched into his jacket and headed for the barn and stables. Beside him, Boston's tags jingled like music as the big dog jumped from snow pile to snow pile.

Inside the barn, warmth engulfed him and the scents of hay and horses welcomed him. Here was the peace he'd built for himself. Here was where his world made sense. Boston ran the length of the center aisle and dropped to the ground beside Jake's grandfather, standing at one of the stalls.

A jolt of anger shook Jake. He stalked across the distance separating them and finally stopped alongside the older man.

Ben didn't even look at him. "Charlie tells me the boy looks just like you. Can't wait to see him."

"You knew." Betrayal was a living, breathing pain in his chest. This old man had been one of the centers of Jake's life. When he'd come home from war, he'd come to this ranch—as much for the steadiness of this man as for the peace of the mountains. "You knew and didn't say a damn word."

Ben scrubbed a hand over the back of his neck and squinted up at Jake. "I knew when your mother found out. Couple days is all."

"It's more warning than I've had." Jake gritted his teeth. "You should have told me."

"Thought about it."

"Doesn't count."

"Your mother thought this way was best."

"My *mother* wants to take that baby away from his mother."

Ben snorted. "Your mother wants *you* to step up for that baby."

Stunned and insulted, Jake stared at him. Did his family really think so little of him? Did they actually believe that he wouldn't do the right thing by his own blood?

"I didn't know about him. Hard to step up for something when you have no idea it exists."

"Well, now you know." Ben's still sharp eyes narrowed on him. "What're you gonna do about it?"

"Wish to hell people would stop asking me that," Jake muttered.

Cass was still feeling jumpy hours later.

Sure, thanks to Jake she didn't have to worry about any plans his mother might have to try to take Luke from her. But now she had to deal with Jake.

"How'd he take it?" Claudia asked.

"Stunned. Shocked." *Angry,* she added silently. Clutching the phone a little tighter to her ear, Cass kept her voice low, since Luke was sleeping in a crib beside her. "He wasn't happy, let's put it that way."

"But after you explained…"

"I didn't get the chance," Cass admitted with a sigh as she dropped onto the window seat and stared out at the view she'd been dreaming about for months. "After he called his mother, he walked out. He hasn't been back to the house since."

"So, drama queen meets drama king," Claudia mused. "A match made in, well, okay. Maybe not heaven."

Rolling her eyes, Cass countered, "Easy enough for you to take this so lightly. It's not your life."

"I'm not taking it lightly," Claud argued. "But Cass, you couldn't just go on forever not telling him. And you know it."

"Maybe," she admitted. Far off in the distance, dark clouds roiled, twisting in the wind, moving ever closer. "But I don't like being pushed into it, either."

"Look on the bright side," her sister said. "Hard part's over. He knows about Luke. Now you just have to work it out between you."

"That *is* the hard part. He's not even talking to me, Claudia. He's—" She broke off and stared as Jake and his dog emerged from the barn and headed for the house. The big yellow dog jumped and rolled in the snow drifts like a clown and Jake looked fierce. Seemed his mood hadn't improved any in the hours since she'd seen him last.

"He's what?"

"He's coming," Cass told her sister. "I've got to go."

"Okay, good luck!"

She was going to need it. Over the last few hours, Cass had been settling into the room she'd used when she was here the last time—at least the room that had been hers until she'd begun staying in Jake's bedroom. Of course, that wasn't going to happen this time. She hadn't come back here for sex.

Her body tingled and she frowned.

Just thinking about sex with Jake was enough to make her body hum and her brain shut down. But she needed to be able to think rationally. To talk to Jake and make him understand why she'd done what she'd done. To tell him what her plans were for their son.

And then, she had to get out of Montana. This time for good.

Downstairs, she heard the kitchen door slam and shivered. He was inside now and probably headed for her. So she stood up, squared her shoulders and lifted her chin. A quick glance into the crib had her smiling. Sleeping soundly, her son was in his favorite position, sprawled spread-eagle, much like his father. As she watched, Luke reached for a tuft of his own black hair and rubbed it between his fingertips.

Her heart filled to bursting and her spine straightened. There was nothing she wouldn't do for this baby. No one she wouldn't face. Nothing she wouldn't dare.

Cass *felt* Jake before she heard him. The man still moved like a ghost, and she wondered if that came naturally to him or if it was a holdover from his time in the military. Either way, it didn't matter once she turned her head to look at him, framed in the open doorway. The yellow Lab slipped past him and went first to Cass, his nails clicking on the hardwood. After she'd given him a pat, the dog stuck his nose between the rails of the crib, snuffled, then lay down right beside it, as if taking up guard duty for the tiny boy inside.

Jake, though, didn't come in, just looked at her, then shifted his gaze to the crib and the sleeping baby. "Where'd you find the crib?"

His voice, though low, was rough and harsh.

"Anna had Charlie bring it down from your attic. She said your grandfather stored the family stuff up there and that you wouldn't mind Luke using your old crib."

"It's fine." His features tightened and a muscle in his jaw clenched. "You should have told me."

Cass flushed and she felt the heat of it sting her cheeks. She could give him excuses, tell him the rationalizations that she'd run through in her mind over and over during the time they'd been apart. Heck, she'd even rehearsed exactly what she would say on the plane ride out here. But now that it was time... now that she was looking into his lake-blue eyes, she couldn't do it.

The simple truth was, he was right. She should have told him from the first. Should have shared the miracle of their son right from the beginning. It had been wrong not to. Her brother and sister had tried to convince her of that, but her own fears had kept her from realizing it.

For so long now, she'd been on her own with Luke, seeing his first smile, his first tooth, and not being able to share it with the one other person who should have been there. There really was no excuse for not telling him—there was only her fears.

"I know."

Surprise flickered in his eyes. "Didn't expect that."

The light was going, sun setting, and with any luck, Luke would sleep through till morning. He'd had a very long day with no nap and too many changes in his routine.

Cass knew the talk she and Jake were about to have was long overdue, but she didn't want to have it here, where they might wake up their son. She gave a look to where the dog lay prone beside the crib, then glanced at Jake. "Is it all right for the dog to stay here?"

"Looks like he already figures Luke is his," Jake told her. "Boston."

The dog lifted his head from his paws.

"Stay."

That heavy yellow tail thumped twice on the floor and then Boston closed his eyes for a nap.

"Good boy." Cass bent down to pet the dog again and then stood to walk to where Jake waited. There was no more putting it off. It was well past time they said what had to be said.

Jake turned in the doorway so she could pass him and as she did, her breasts brushed against his chest. Sparks of awareness, of need, lit up her insides and she had to take a deep breath to steady herself. God, it had been so long since she'd felt that quickening of her pulse. The hot rush of desire churning through her insides.

She looked up at him and knew he'd felt that same electrical jolt—and he didn't look any happier about it than she felt at the moment. "Jake—"

"Not here." He took her elbow in one palm and led her to the next door down the hall, to his room. Once inside, he closed the door partially, leaving it open just wide enough that they would be able to hear the baby if he stirred.

Strangely, that small action caused her heart to ping with tenderness. Then the moment was past and she was watching him stride across the master bedroom toward the wall of windows that overlooked a wide, snow-covered forest and Whitefish Lake, its sapphire-blue surface covered in snow and ice. "Explain."

"Jake—"

He turned to face her, his features grim, his luscious mouth tight and firm. "Explain to me why you never bothered to use a damn phone. Why you thought

I wouldn't want to know that you were carrying my son."

Cass winced under that blow, but a part of her knew she deserved it. She looked at him and didn't see only the righteous anger she'd been prepared for, but she also saw pain. Pain she'd caused because she'd been too much of a coward to face him with the truth.

And while she could admit to all of that, in her defense, he'd made no secret of the fact that he wasn't interested in family. Was it wrong that she'd taken him at his word?

"You're the one who told me you were a loner. You didn't want family around."

"I didn't say I wouldn't want my *son*," he said, each word dropping like an ice cube between them.

"No, you didn't," she agreed, walking farther into the room. She tried not to look at that wide bed where they'd spent so many hours tangled together. Because the memories were already so rich, they were cluttering her mind, making it difficult to think straight. "But we agreed that what we had was temporary, Jake."

"It was. Luke isn't."

"No, he's not. He's precious and wonderful and I don't want him to be a burden you're forced to pick up and carry because you're an honorable man." And she couldn't risk having her son grow to count on his father, depend on him, only to be shattered if Jake suddenly decided that he wasn't interested in a family anymore.

"So you get to decide for me? Is that it?" He turned his face from hers briefly, staring out at the sky and the blustering wind.

"I thought it would be easier. On all of us."

He whipped his head around to glare at her. "You thought wrong."

"Yeah. I can see that." She walked past the bed and didn't stop until she was standing right in front of him. "If you want to know your son, that's great. But I'm not expecting anything from you, Jake."

"Well, I'm expecting plenty." His eyes were on fire with emotions. She felt his body nearly vibrating with everything that he was keeping locked down, locked away.

The room was filled with shadows. The last of the sun had faded as they talked. A half moon was rising, fighting to shine in spite of the dark storm clouds rushing across the sky. Wind rattled the windows as Jake demanded, "What's his name? His *last* name."

Cass frowned, prepared for battle. He wouldn't like this, but it had been her decision to make, after all.

"Moore." Before he could speak, she said, "You're listed on his birth certificate as his father, but I thought it would be easier if my son and I had the same last name."

"Agreed," he said, reaching out for her and pulling her tightly to him. "Only difference is, that last name is going to be Hunter."

Shocked nearly speechless, it took Cass a moment to recover before she blurted, "Excuse me?"

"Welcome home, Mrs. Hunter."

Eight

Jake's belly clenched as soon as he said the words.

Hell, who could blame him? The last time he'd asked a woman to marry him, it had turned into a major disaster. Jake had vowed to never repeat that mistake. To keep to himself. To never risk letting someone get too close again.

Yet what choice did he have? His son was sleeping in the other room. He'd made a child and now it was time to do the right thing. Marry that child's mother.

Even as he considered the situation, he reassured himself that this proposal wasn't about love. He still wouldn't be letting Cassie get under his skin. *On* his skin was something else. And that consideration eased the skittering panic in his brain. Sex with Cassie was amazing. Hadn't he been missing it for nearly a year and a half?

Marrying her would ensure that he could have her all the damn time and that was a huge plus.

Not to mention his son would be *here* on the ranch, where he belonged. Through the confused thoughts came one image, that of his little boy, racing across the ranch yard, with Boston at his heels. Damned if that didn't bring a smile to his face. Until Cassie started talking again.

"Are you crazy?"

Not the reaction most men got with a proposal.

"No."

"That's it? Just 'no'?"

She stared at him for a long minute or two, neither of them speaking as shadows crept from the corners of the room like thieves, stealing the last of the light.

Jake studied her in the dimness and felt more than his belly clench. His groin was hard and aching and everything in him yearned to hold her tighter, closer. Yeah, he wanted her. In spite of the anger over her keeping his son from him. In spite of everything, he wanted her. Would *always* want her. But damned if he'd admit that to her.

When she pulled free of his grasp, he let her go. Only so far, though.

"I'm not going to marry you, Jake."

He crossed his arms over his chest and planted his feet wide apart in a "ready for a fight" stance. "Don't see a way around it."

"None of that cowboy-speak, either. Use full sentences."

"Fine," he said, moving in on her. "You want lots of words? Here are a few for you. You kept my son from me. You kept his existence a secret. You think

I'm just going to say thanks for dropping by so I could get a look at him? Not a chance. That boy's a Hunter and he stays here. Where he belongs."

She blinked and shook her head. "He belongs with me."

"There you go." He waved one hand. "That's why the marriage. He's going to have a mother and a father."

"I told you I didn't want Luke to be the burden of honor that you picked up because it was the right thing to do," she countered, moving in on him now, poking him dead center of the chest with the tip of her index finger to emphasize each word. "Well, I won't be your duty, either. I know you don't want a family and I'm not going to sign on to be your wife out of obligation. No thanks."

Anger erupted. Not surprising since it had been there, deep inside him, bubbling, churning, demanding release, since she'd first walked into his house carrying that baby. Emotions he'd thought long buried were swimming to the surface, but he didn't want to look at them now. There were too many of them and he was in no position to try to sort through every feeling that was knocking around his heart demanding to be recognized.

He couldn't let the anger or the emotions guide him right now. Instead, he grabbed for a single, slender thread of logic and clung to it.

His gaze fixed on hers, and he willed her to hear. To understand. "You say 'duty' like it's a dirty word. It's not. Duty means you accept responsibility for what you've done. It's making a personal vow to do what's right. What's necessary. It's an obligation to face what others can't or won't. Duty means something to me, Cassie, and I can't change that. Even for you."

"I don't expect you to change," she argued, looking up at him, her emotions churning in the fog of her eyes. "I'm not asking you to. Just as I'm not going to marry a man who thinks of me as an obligation."

He snorted. "Not an obligation, Cassie," he said, "a thorn. An attractive thorn that I wouldn't mind tossing onto my bed about now, but still a thorn."

She had been just that right from the start. A thorn jabbed into his skin, painful and irritating until he pulled it out and still felt the ache. Cassie had wedged herself into his life, made him nuts while she was here on the ranch, and then made him full-on crazy once she left. Now she was back and he couldn't make sense of anything he was feeling, thinking.

The only thing he knew for sure was that he wanted her. Bad. His desire for her hadn't waned a damn bit while they were apart and he knew now it never would.

"Wow. Be still my heart." Shaking her head slowly, she said, "That's even less incentive to marry you, Jake."

"You want incentive? What about our son?" God, that felt weird to say. Weird to know that he was a *father*. "What does he deserve?"

"He deserves to be loved," Cassie said quickly, decisively. "And cared for. And not thought of as a cross to bear."

That flash of anger burned a little brighter. Did she really think him so small that he couldn't love his own child? No, he hadn't planned on having a family, trusting fate to keep them safe so he wouldn't have his heart ripped out, but now that the choice had been made for him, he wouldn't wish it away.

"You don't get to say that to me, Cassie. How old is he?"

"Almost five months."

Jake gritted his teeth. "You've had him five months and knew about him for nine before that. You've had the chance to love him. I've barely caught a glimpse of him. So don't be telling me that I won't love my son."

"I don't want you to *have* to love him. Don't you see the difference?"

"If you had told me about him from the jump there wouldn't be any worries about 'having' to love him, would there?"

She threw her hands in the air. "How do I know that? How do *you?* If I had called you when I first found out, would you have wanted the baby?"

He swallowed hard past the knot of emotion clogging his throat. Cassie latched onto that moment of hesitation.

"See? You don't even know how you would've reacted, and I couldn't take the chance. Not with my baby's future happiness at stake."

"I deserved to know," he finally said, not bothering to counter her arguments because at the heart of it, he was right and she was wrong and he had a feeling she knew that as well as he did.

All of the fight went out of her like air sliding from a balloon. "You did. You really did. And I'm sorry."

Nodding, he looked down at her and felt resolution settle into his soul. He wouldn't say he loved her because how the hell did he know what love was? But he could admire her. Respect her. Desire her. She'd been a single mom and she'd done a good job. Luke looked healthy and happy and that was due to her. He had no idea what her life had been like over the last fourteen months, but he knew what his had been. Enduring endless nights, where he cursed the solitude he used to crave. Spending the days doing what he always had, never once guessing that a piece of him was living and growing without him.

She had been strong and he could appreciate that. But now things had changed. Now she was here, and he wasn't letting her go again. There was only one way this was going to end. *His* way.

"Yeah, well, I'm sorry too, Cassie."

She flicked him a sideways look, wary and suspicious. "Sorry for what?"

Jake cupped her chin in his fingers and felt that buzz of connection that he'd felt the very first time he touched her. He held her so that she was forced to meet his gaze, forced to see in his eyes that he meant everything he said next. "You don't have to worry about my mother anymore. But I'll tell you this. You either marry me, or I'll sue you for custody myself."

Cass pulled out of his touch and the tips of his fingers still felt warm from the contact with her skin.

Eyes wide, breath hitching in her chest, she said, "You wouldn't do that."

"Watch me," he promised, even as he acknowledged objectively that the Hunters were a damned vindictive family. Even him. She'd wanted him to save her from his mother and now she was finding out that the price for that favor was surrendering to him. He wouldn't have thought himself capable of threatening a woman—especially *this* woman—but it seemed the surprises of the day were still coming.

"I won't lose my son."

She choked out a laugh, lifted one hand to cover her mouth as if she could push the sound back inside, then looked up at him. "You realize I came to you for help?"

"Ironic," he acknowledged.

Cass walked away from him and dropped down to sit on the edge of his bed. Seeing her there again brought back all the memories he'd been trying to ignore for months. The scent of her on his pillows. The image of her hair, spilling across the sheets. The gleam in her eyes when he filled her with his body and the soft sigh of completion that always touched something deep inside him.

All of those memories and more came crowding back until he nearly choked on them. He'd been fine with his world before she came here and got trapped for a week. And after she left, he worked damned hard to be fine again. Hadn't really happened, but he'd been moving toward some sort of peace until she showed up again.

When she looked at him, she said softly, "So basically, I went from the frying pan into the fire?"

"Yeah."

She laughed shortly and shook her head. "One word. Typical."

Sighing, Jake let the anger within dissipate. He'd learned long ago to accept what had already happened because he couldn't change it. He'd lost so much time with his son that he'd never get back, but that was done.

All he could do now was ensure that he wouldn't lose any more of his child's life.

He walked over, sat down beside her and took a breath, dragging her scent into his lungs. "Were you ever going to tell me about Luke?"

Her hands twisted in her lap as she admitted, "I don't know."

Nodding, he briefly shifted his gaze to the window and the night. "What happened to forthright?"

Cass looked at him. "If lies will protect my son, then that's what I'll do."

"You think he needs to be protected? From me?" Insult stabbed at him.

"It's my job to make sure Luke is happy. Safe. Loved," she said, not really answering the question.

The room was dark so that he could hardly see her, and maybe that was best. If he read fear or worry or anything remotely like that in her eyes, he might soften. Might relent. And he couldn't.

He wasn't going to lose his son, so Cassie had best make up her mind to be his wife.

"We'll do that. Together."

"I'm not going to marry you, Jake."

"Your choice," he said softly. "But you're not going anywhere, Cassie."

"I'm not a prisoner," she countered. "You can't make me stay here if I want to go, Jake."

"Oh, I could. Make no mistake. As it turns out though, I won't have to." He pointed at the wall of windows and the dark winter beyond the glass. "There's a severe storm warning for this area for the next five days. A blizzard's going to hit and it's gonna be a big one. So settle in, Cassie. You and Luke are going nowhere."

* * *

The wind screamed for hours.

Like the shriek of lost souls, it wound itself around the house, as if frustrated at not being able to find a way in. Just as Cassie couldn't find a way out.

Physically, she was good and trapped here. Once the snow started falling, she knew she could never risk traveling on that terrifying mountain road. It would be one thing to risk her own safety, but no way would she strap her son into a car and hope for the best.

But emotionally, she was trapped even more neatly. For almost a year and a half, she'd done her best to forget about Jake. To put him on a shelf in her mind so that she wasn't constantly tormented by the memories of the week she'd had with him. But with Luke looking more and more like his father every day, forgetting wasn't easy.

She'd even begun to question if she really wanted to forget. Cass had wondered constantly if she'd done the right thing in keeping Luke a secret from his father—though there was no changing that decision. Now she was back with a man who was both furious and determined to get her to marry him.

How could she do that, though? Marry a man who didn't love her? Wasn't marriage a risk even *with* love?

Cass had seen her parents' marriage erode into rubble and she still had the emotional scars to prove it. She couldn't set her own child up for the kind of hurt she'd once known. Sure, Jake was positive he wanted her and Luke here now. But what about a year from now? Five years? What if he one day decided he'd had enough and sent them away?

How could she live with herself knowing that she'd

brought Luke the kind of pain no child should ever know? The pain of knowing that your parent didn't want you.

To make matters worse, she couldn't *sleep.*

Luke wasn't the problem. He'd been sleeping through the night since he was two months old, bless him. No, it was her own mind that was keeping her awake. Thoughts of Jake refused to quiet down and go away.

This was not how she had expected her trip to Montana to go. Cass had been prepared for Jake's anger, but the thought that *he* might now want to take custody of Lucas had never occurred to her. As for the proposal, that hadn't been real and they both knew it. He was just angry—he had a right, she could admit that—but he didn't want *her,* he wanted his son.

He couldn't have Luke.

Even sharing her son was going to be hard at first. After all, since Luke's birth, Cass had been on her own, doing everything herself. Yes, that was her own doing, but the fact remained that things were going to be changing now.

Remembering the last of their conversation hours before, she cringed.

"I know you believe that proposing to me is the right thing to do," she said, struggling to keep a calmness she wasn't feeling in her voice, *"and I appreciate the thought. But this isn't the 1950s and I don't need you to step in and save my reputation. Luke and I are doing fine on our own."*

"But you're not on your own anymore, Cassie," he said, voice as dark as the shadows crouched in his eyes. *"There's me to contend with, too. And I don't*

*give a flying damn about some fifties ideal. I asked
you to marry me because you're the mother of my son
and I figured you'd rather be where he is."*

"I will be. In Boston."

"Montana. Get used to it."

How was she supposed to get used to an ultimatum?

She flipped onto her side, facing the crib and the
wall of windows, and punched at her pillow. It wouldn't
help her sleep, but it took care of a little of the frustration clawing at her.

How could you argue with a man who spoke in
two-word sentences?

But he'd had more to say today, hadn't he? And
then the proposal? Her stomach swam with nerves
and…pleasure?

Oh, God. She slapped one hand to her forehead.
How could she even pretend to enjoy that dogmatic de-
mand for marriage? She had to be as crazy as he was.

Desire was one thing, she told herself firmly—letting it get out of hand was something else. She had
to remember what was important here. Luke. That's
why she'd come back to Montana. Keeping her son
safe had been the goal.

Though now she had to worry about Jake's trying to
get custody, so had she really ensured Luke's safety?

When the door to her bedroom opened quietly, a
spear of light from the hallway slanted across her bed,
lighting up the darkness. She didn't turn to look. She
didn't have to. She could *feel* Jake's presence. What
she didn't know was what he wanted. But she'd had
enough of arguing for the night, so she feigned sleep,
not moving a muscle as he stepped into her room.

The door remained open and the light looked like a

golden slash through the shadows. He moved so softly, all she heard was the whisper of his jean-clad thighs. Holding her breath, she waited to see what he would do. If he came to her, if he kissed her, Cass knew she'd be lost. All of these months without his touch left her vulnerable to his slightest caress.

But he didn't come to her. Instead, he walked to the crib. Cass heard Boston's tail thump against the floor before Jake shushed him with a quiet command. Cass looked at the man in the shadows and watched as he bent low over the crib, reaching down to the sleeping baby. She saw him smooth his work-roughened hand over his son's head and her heart twisted at that gentle action.

"Hello, Luke," Jake whispered in hardly more than an expelled breath. "I'm your father. You don't know me yet. But I promise you will."

Luke snuffled and made the little squeaky sound that always made Cass think he was dreaming.

Jake watched the sleeping boy for what felt like hours. Cass's heart ached for the man and for herself. She was in serious trouble here and she knew it. Because the simple truth was, she loved Jake Hunter—a man determined to keep his heart locked away behind a wall of his own making.

Then finally, as quietly as he'd arrived, he left her room, shutting the door behind him.

By morning, the wind had died down a little and the sky looked as if it had been cast out of molten silver. Huge clouds settled over the mountain, looking as though they might drop right out of the sky any minute. It was cold, too, but Cassie had Luke bundled against the weather, zipped into his baby snow sack. When she carried him outside and stepped off the porch, she gulped in a breath of air that was so cold it felt like icicles being shoved down her throat. She probably should have stayed in the house, but she wanted to talk to Ben, and making an old man come out in the cold seemed mean somehow.

It only took a few seconds to walk across the yard to Ben's cabin, and as she got closer, she noticed that Jake's grandfather had a Christmas tree set up in the front window. The lights on it glowed in the shadowy day, looking cheerful enough to make her smile even after a long, sleepless night.

Ben opened the door before she could knock and swept her and Luke inside. Warmth wrapped itself around her and Cass sighed in appreciation.

"You shouldn't have come out in this cold, Cassie girl," Ben was saying as he adeptly lifted Luke out of her arms.

"I will admit that it's nice to be inside. Even that short walk is really cold."

"Blizzard's coming in fast," he said, with a quick glance out the window at the sky. "Best you two don't stay long and get back to the main house."

"Will you be all right over here by yourself in a blizzard?"

He laughed at that and set the baby more easily on his forearm. "Cassie, I've lived through more Montana blizzards than you could count. Got plenty of food, plenty of firewood, and just in case, I've got the generator. Jake installed a top-of-the-line generator at the main house and every cabin here when he took over. Trust me, we're set." He shrugged. "Besides, I've got a front-row seat and I kinda like watching it when the storm starts getting mean."

Cass smiled. "Jake's a lot like you, isn't he?"

"Only if that's a good thing," Ben replied with a wink. "I know things are rough going between you two right now, Cassie. But Jake's a good man. He'll do the right by you."

"That's the problem," she admitted, her heart sinking at yet more evidence that Jake Hunter would pick up his sack of troubles—Cass and Luke—and carry on stoically. "He'll do the right thing even if he doesn't want to."

"You think he doesn't want to?" Ben laughed, and led the way into the front room, fully expecting her to follow him. "You young people sure are blind sometimes. Wonder if it's on purpose?"

"If what's on purpose?" she asked.

"Nothing, nothing." The older man turned Luke in his arms so he could see the tiny face staring back at him and Ben gave the boy a wide grin. "A great-grandson. Isn't that something, though?"

A ping of guilt hit her hard and Cass told herself she had more people than just Jake to apologize to. She'd kept Luke from his family and she had the distinct feeling that guilt was going to be with her for quite a while. "I'm sorry, Ben. I should have told you and Jake and even Elise a long time ago."

Ben's sharp blue eyes fixed on her. "I expect you had your reasons."

"I did," she admitted as she slipped out of her coat. "They even made sense until I got here and talked to Jake."

Ben chuckled and carried Luke across the front room. "Well, you two will work things out eventually."

He sat down in a big leather recliner, balancing Luke on his lap. Ben's big, work-worn, time-weathered hands held the baby as gently as he might have a wounded bird. The little boy squirmed excitedly until his snowsuit was unzipped and he was freed from captivity. Then he pushed himself up on wobbly legs and braced his small hands against his great-grandfather's chest. Eyes met, smiles were exchanged and in the span of moments, Cass watched as love was born.

It hurt to admit that she'd been cheating her son out of the love that was his due. His right. She'd cheated all of them and didn't have a clue how she could make up for it.

She took a seat nearby and looked at Ben's Christmas tree. It filled the house with a luscious scent and sparkled and shone like a new morning.

Christmas. Luke's first.

"It's a beautiful tree."

"Jake goes out and cuts me down the perfect one, every year."

"But he doesn't get one for himself?"

Frowning, the older man sat Luke on his lap again and gave the boy his pocket watch to play with. "Jake hasn't celebrated Christmas in so long, he might not even know how to anymore."

Now it was her turn to frown. She'd wondered why there hadn't been any sign of Christmas in the ranch house. Of course, a man alone wouldn't do much decorating, but she had been surprised that Anna hadn't put out pine boughs and lights and things. Now she understood the barrenness of the main house. "Do you know why?"

"He never told me."

"Secrets and shadows," she murmured, turning back to the tree where lights burned brightly and strings of silver tinsel caught the reflections of that light and spun it out again. Across the yard, the main house looked dark and forgotten in comparison to the hopeful joy of Ben's tree. "I can't stay with him."

She didn't know why she'd said it. Probably shouldn't have, but Jake's grandfather had been a friend to her before and she desperately needed one now.

"Too early to give up, Cassie."

"Is it?" She looked at her son and then at the older man. "Should I stay and try and then fail? Should I let Luke fall in love with his father and then have his heart broken when we eventually go our separate ways?"

"Why do you young people always think about divorce?"

"I didn't—"

"Seems to me that when you're talking about getting married, then you should be thinking about succeeding, not failing. Why go into *anything* if you believe you'll fail?"

"He doesn't want to marry me, Ben. He only wants his son."

"Can you blame him for that?"

"Of course not, but—"

"I think you two have to find a way to reach common ground," he said, like a diplomat. "But it won't happen if you shut each other out."

She laughed shortly. "He never let me in."

Ben winked at her. "He got a dog, didn't he?"

"What?"

"The dog. Always said he didn't want one," Ben mused. "Said a house dog was too much trouble and too much time. But you hadn't been gone a week when he brought that puppy home."

"That doesn't mean—"

Ben's white eyebrows lifted. "Called him Boston, too."

True, she had thought that maybe he'd named the dog that because of her. But as Jake made a point of telling her, *he* was also originally from Boston.

"That's where he was born," Cass said, shaking her head more firmly. "His family lives there."

"Uh-huh, and he's spent most of his adult life trying to break away from Boston," Ben reminded her. "The only reason I figure he gave the dog the name of a city he can't stand is because of you. Because he couldn't forget you, and more—didn't want to forget."

Hope jumped to life in one small corner of her heart. If Ben was right, maybe there was a chance. Maybe she and Jake could find a way past their own doubts and fears and make this work. *If* Ben was right.

When she left here the last time she had been half in love with him. Seeing him with Luke last night in her room had given her that extra shove she'd needed, though Cass knew that love alone wouldn't be enough. Could she trust him to stay? Could she believe that a happy ending was possible?

"Would you mind looking after Luke for a little while?" Cass stood up and pulled her coat back on.

"Not a bit. What've you got up your sleeve, Cassie?"

She wasn't sure. Heck, she wasn't sure of much

anymore, it seemed. But she did know that she was here now and if she didn't at least try to get through to Jake, she might spend the rest of her life regretting it.

"I'm hoping there's magic up my sleeve."

Nine

Jake was cold to the bone and exhausted.

Several hours out on the land in a driving, icy wind would do that to a man. Of course, the exhaustion probably had a lot to do with the fact that he hadn't gotten any sleep the night before. With Cassie in the room right next door to him, he'd lain awake, tormented by thoughts and images of her.

The anger that had burned so brightly the day before was now just smoldering embers. Yes, he could understand what she'd done and even why—he hadn't exactly shown her the picture of a man interested in family when she was here the last time. But knowing how much of his son's life he'd already missed cut at him harder than any icy wind. What he had to decide was what to do now.

He knew what he wanted. He wanted Cassie. Now more than ever.

And he wanted his son.

But the man he'd become wasn't exactly good material for building a happily ever after.

Jake stabled his horse, gave it a good rubdown and made sure it and the other animals in the barn had plenty of feed and water before heading for the main house.

The blizzard was finally kicking in, Jake thought as he stepped from the shelter of the stable into a wind strong enough to knock a man down. Wrapping his right arm around the rope stretched across the yard, he made his way to the main house. The snow was flying and with every step he took, the flakes came faster, thicker, until even squinting, he could barely see the porch he was aimed for. It was as if the storm had waited for him and the ranch hands to return before cutting itself loose. He finally reached the porch, stomped most of the snow off and gratefully stepped inside.

Warmth reached for him and Jake took a deep breath, then released it on a sigh. Grateful to be out of the cold, it took him a second to realize that the scent of pine permeated the house.

"What the hell?"

He shrugged out of his jacket, tossed his hat and scarf onto a nearby hook, then stomped through the entryway into the main room, looking for the source of that smell.

Everyone on the ranch knew he didn't do Christmas. Didn't do trees. So he knew Anna wouldn't have brought anything into the house. Which left Cassie. Though how she would have managed—

His thoughts broke off. There was no tree in the room, just boughs of pine branches lining the fireplace mantel and stuck behind picture frames. There was a vase filled with pine branches, and the roaring fire heated the scent, saturating the air until it was rich and thick.

"You're back."

His gaze snapped to the woman sitting on the floor in front of the wide windows. Her hair was long and loose around her shoulders and her smile when she looked at him sent heat sliding through him. It had been a long, hard, cold day, but coming home to that smile was something a man could get used to.

Backlit by the growing storm, Cassie looked impossibly young and beautiful as she sat opposite Luke, with Boston sprawled on the floor beside them. As he watched, the baby slapped both hands onto the dog's broad back and rocked unsteadily from side to side, grinning wildly when he'd completed the task. An answering smile of pride touched Jake's mouth briefly. How was it possible that such a tiny human being could turn a man's heart inside out?

Boston's tail thumped in appreciation.

"This is the best dog," Cassie said, her voice breaking the spell holding him in place as she reached out one hand to stroke Boston's head. "He just loves Luke to pieces."

"Yeah, he does." She and the baby were taking over his home, his life. Hell, even his dog had abandoned him in favor of Luke. Jake's gaze swept around the room, taking in the rest of the pine decorations until he spotted a nativity scene on the coffee table. He hadn't seen it since he was a boy. "Where did you find that?"

Cassie pushed herself to her feet, picked Luke up and wandered over as if she had all the time in the world. As if she hadn't noticed the tightness in Jake's voice.

"In the attic," she said with a smile, setting Luke down in front of the hand-carved wooden pieces. Instantly, the little boy picked up a sheep and started gnawing on it. "It was Ben's idea. He said that all of the old family decorations were up there and I should help myself to what I could find."

His own grandfather. Still working against him. Ben liked Cassie, and now that Luke was involved too, the older man was making no secret of the fact that he wanted them to stay. Well hell, so did Jake. But he had more at risk than Ben did, so Jake had to look at the situation from all angles.

He took another pine-scented breath and tried to still the rumblings inside him, his gaze fixed on the long-forgotten nativity. Ben had carved that set himself when Jake's mother was just a girl. When he was a kid, Jake had done the same things that Luke was doing now. Funny, he hadn't thought about that nativity set in years. But then, he didn't spend a lot of time thinking about the past or Christmas in particular.

Still, he watched Luke move the cows and sheep around on the table and he found himself smiling again.

"Good. You don't mind that I set it up. Luke loves it. He's been playing with it all afternoon." Then she looked up at him and seemed to see him for the first time. "You look tired. Are you hungry? Anna left a pot of stew cooking before she went home. She said since the blizzard hadn't hit yet, there was no reason for her to stay."

"Yeah, the men will be out working in this mess tomorrow so Anna will probably spend the next few days cooking here for everyone. So it's good she went home to rest up."

"So many words," Cass said with a smile. "You must be hungry."

"Yeah. Hungry." That was probably the reason his defenses were down enough that he wasn't telling her to take away the pine branches and pack up the nativity. Had to be the reason, he assured himself.

"Come on," she said, scooping up Luke and heading for the kitchen without waiting to see if Jake was following. "You can eat and tell me what it's like out there."

He fell into step behind her and his gaze dropped unerringly to the curve of her behind in her faded jeans. His body tensed and despite the exhaustion pulling at his every cell, he found he might not be *too* tired. Whatever else lay between them, there was passion, bright and burning and damned hard to ignore.

Shaking his head, he walked into the kitchen and stopped her before she could take down a bowl and spoon. "I can serve myself. You don't have to do it."

Cassie set Luke into a high chair—no doubt also rescued from the attic—strapped him in and said, "I don't mind. You've been out in this mess all day." She glanced out the window at the wall of snow getting thicker by the minute and shivered. "Sit down."

He sat beside his son and kept his gaze locked on the boy because he figured that was safer than watching Cassie making herself at home in his kitchen. Memories of Lisa and his failed marriage rushed up to nearly choke him. He didn't remember a single time that Lisa had come to the kitchen to serve herself. His memories of her were more about what others could do for her. At Christmastime especially, it had been about gifts she expected, the more expensive the better. She never would have gone into the attic after an old nativity set. Never would have strung pine branches around the house.

Cassie wasn't like her, he told himself, and yet the mistrust was still there. He was waiting, he knew, for Cassie to fail. To show him that underneath her facade, she was another Lisa. She was another invitation to misery. Cassie had come into his life, turned it upside down and shaken it like a child's snow globe, and then left—only to return with a baby she hadn't bothered to tell him about.

Didn't that prove that she couldn't be trusted?

His heart iced over as he watched her. He couldn't afford to trust again. Couldn't risk making another huge mistake. And yet…there was Luke to consider in all this. His son. Jake wouldn't lose the boy—so that meant finding a way to deal with his mother.

Cassie was humming under her breath as she moved about the room and Jake's instincts went on high alert. She was too damn cheerful. Here she was, trapped at the ranch, and judging by the strength of this storm she wasn't going anywhere for quite a while. Yet she was humming. Acting as though she was happy. Why?

"Ben tells me you went out to lay down hay for the cattle before the storm hit."

"Yeah. Made it back here just in time, too." He

ran one hand through his hair and handed the baby a cracker from the tray on the table. Smiling to himself, he watched as Luke took a big bite and then reached over the edge of the chair to try to share with Boston. Better, he thought, to talk about ranch business, the storm—anything other than what lay between them.

Sighing a little, he explained, "Rather than dig through snow to find grass, cattle will just stand there and starve to death. We laid out hay near a series of caves that will give them shelter if they want it. Best we can do for now." He glanced out the window and hissed in a breath at the sight of a white wall flying horizontally past the glass.

Mid-afternoon and it was dark outside. He couldn't see the lights from Ben's house or the other cabins. The storm was a big one and was bound to get even worse. "After I eat, I'll check the generator again, make sure it's good to go if the power gets knocked out."

"Ben and one of the guys did that earlier while you were gone," she told him as she served up a bowl of stew that smelled like heaven. "They checked every one of them and they're all good. Ben says you bought top-of-the-line generators to make sure everyone would stay warm during a power outage."

Even as pleased as he was at the prospect of a meal, he felt a stab of irritation that she was so at home here. She was close with his grandfather. Had made friends with Anna and the hands who worked on the ranch. He'd seen it for himself the last time she was here. Again, one word echoed in his mind. *Why?*

Pushing all of his doubts aside for the moment, Jake picked up a spoon and dug in, relishing the warmth that spilled through him at the first bite. When he'd eaten half a bowlful, he glanced up at Cassie, who sat opposite him. Time to get a few things clear. Let her know that she couldn't just rearrange his house and life as she wanted.

"Maybe you didn't know this, but I don't celebrate Christmas."

"I know," she said, handing Luke another cracker. "Ben told me."

"Ben's got a lot to say."

"In fairly long sentences, too," she added with a quirk of her lips.

He sighed, then his gaze fixed briefly on her mouth and the memory of the taste of her swamped him. She was the one woman he couldn't forget. The one he couldn't stop wanting. And the one who could make his life the hardest—just by being her.

"If you knew how I felt," he blurted out, "why all the pine?"

"I didn't put up a tree," she pointed out, then reached across to smooth Luke's hair back from his face.

"That's not what I asked."

Shaking her head, she looked at Jake. "This is Luke's first Christmas and my first Christmas away from my brother and sister. Until we can get back to Boston—" the dog looked up hopefully "—I'm going to do what I can here."

Back to Boston.

Those three words wiped out any other argument he might have made about the Christmas decorations. A sinking sensation opened up in his gut. It felt as cold as the storm raging outside the warmth of the house.

The thought of Cassie's leaving wasn't something he was willing to consider. Whether she liked it or not, she was staying. So before anything else was said, they had to get this one thing straight between them.

"You're not going back," he told her, his gaze locked on hers, so he saw the flare of outrage spark in those gray eyes. "At least, no time soon. So you might as well put through a call to whoever you work for and tell them you're gone until at least January."

She stiffened in her chair. "You can't order me around, Jake."

"Just did." He set his spoon in the bowl and though he'd like more of that stew, this conversation had priority. "I want time with the son I just found out I had."

She flinched. Good. Even better if she really thought he was willing to let her leave come January, because it would keep her defenses down. The truth was, he would do whatever he had to do to make sure that she and Luke never left this ranch. He might not be husband and father material, but that didn't matter anymore, did it? Trust each other or not, the two of them were linked by a son they both wanted. For now, that would be enough.

Sighing, Cassie said, "I work for myself. From home. I do billing for several small companies in Boston."

Again, that tail thumped against the floor.

"Good. So you can stay with no worries." He carried his bowl to the sink and rinsed it out. Turning, he braced both hands on the counter behind him and looked at her. Jake had the feeling he could stare at Cassie forever and never tire of the view.

When that thought sailed through his mind, he told himself he should probably be worried. But he wasn't. He might not trust her completely, but he could admit, at least silently, that she tugged at strings inside him he hadn't even known were there. She was thawing a heart that had been cold for so long, it was a wonder it could beat.

Even when her fog-gray eyes were flashing with indignation, as they were now, she was the most beautiful thing he had ever seen in his life. And he wanted her now more than he wanted to go on living. Everything in him itched to take her. To lose himself in her heat and scent.

"I'll stay," she said shortly as she pushed up from her chair and crossed to him. "For now, anyway."

At least they agreed on that much, Jake told himself, looking down into her eyes, feeling himself fall into that smoky fog.

"But this isn't settled, Jake," she whispered.

Giving in to instinct, Jake reached for her, dragged her close and kissed her, hard and deep. His head swam, his blood rushed and his heartbeat pounded so hard it should have sounded like a drum in the stillness of the room.

She yielded to him, bending her body into his, wrapping her arms around his neck and parting her lips for his tongue. Desire sizzled into a blistering arc between them. When he pulled his head back after what felt like an eternity, he stared at her and agreed, "Not settled."

When his phone rang, Ben picked it up, smiling. "Hello, honey."

"Hi, Dad," Elise said. "How's it going on your end?"

Ben looked through his windows at the main house and imagined the three people inside it. Cassie and

Jake were making this so much harder on themselves than it had to be. Ben had seen for himself what was shining in the air between those two. And with the baby they shared, they had the beginnings of something wonderful—if they chose to take the chance.

"It's…interesting," he finally said, settling into his chair. "That baby is a cutie."

"He is, in the pictures Cass's sister showed me." She sighed a little. "Luke looks just like Jake at that age. I can't believe I have a grandson I've never even met. And now, with Cass as angry at me as she is, who knows when I will meet him?"

"You did the right thing, Elise," Ben told his daughter. "Threatening to take the baby. Jake and Cassie both were too stubborn to see what was right in front of them until they were faced with a common enemy."

"That's me," Elise Hunter said with a sigh. "The enemy."

"It'll work out, honey. Now, let me tell you about your grandson…"

The blizzard raged for the next three days.

Cassie had never seen anything like it. Every time the wind died down long enough for the men to get out and run the snowplows across the yard—as soon as they were finished it all began again. Trees were bent with the weight of the snow on their branches. Drifts piled high against the sides of the ranch buildings and the wind howled. It was like living in the middle of a disaster movie.

And yet, in a weird way, the storm forced a closeness that she and Jake might have spent months building between them otherwise. She worked day and night, just as he and the hands did, catching brief naps whenever she could. She brewed coffee by the gallon, made hundreds of sandwiches and oceans of soup. The men came in and out of the house at all hours, looking for food or just a chance to get out of the wind.

Whenever they showed up, she was ready. There was hot soup, cookies, slow-cooker meals. The kitchen stove never cooled off and she was busier than she'd ever been before, and yet Cassie couldn't remember a time when she'd enjoyed herself more. She was needed here, and seeing approval and surprise in Jake's eyes was as good as a medal to her.

She knew he'd half expected her to sit out the storm hiding in her room or concentrating solely on Luke. But as she jumped in to help, she saw that he was grateful. And that made the hard work worth every minute.

Of course, she also found time to torment him, too. She knew he didn't like Christmas, but she didn't know why. And since he wouldn't talk to her, tell her what he was feeling, she went right on, building Christmas piece by piece. Every night, when he came back to the ranch house, there were more decorations spread around. She found old strings of lights in the attic, and hung them around the main room, draping them over the pine branches. With the generator's help, they cast a multicolored glow over the big room.

In the attic she'd also found an abandoned, threadbare quilt that she'd cut up and, in snatches of time when she wasn't cooking, sewn into Christmas stockings. Three of them. She hung them from the mantel and couldn't help but be proud. And today, with what looked like a break in the storm, she'd liberated an old box of ornaments from the attic. They might not have a tree, but she could hang the decorations from the pine boughs, adding to the determinedly cheerful picture she was trying so hard to create.

"What've you got there?"

Cass jumped, startled, and looked up at Jake as he walked into the great room. She was seated in front of the hearth, where a fire snapped and hissed, sending heat out into the room. The box of ornaments was in front of her and she'd already unwrapped several layers of tissue paper to reveal toy soldiers, a miniature fire engine that Luke would love, and a Christmas star.

"I went up to the attic a little while ago and found this."

"That attic must be about empty by now." Shaking his head, he crouched beside her and picked up the fire engine. The ornament looked even smaller on the palm of his big hand, but he stroked the tip of one finger gently across its chipped paint. "I remember this."

Her heart twisted a little at the tenderness in his eyes and the bemused smile on his face. He kept so much of himself locked away that seeing even a small part of him revealed was like opening a Christmas present and finding exactly what you had hoped for.

As she watched, he eased down to sit on the floor beside her, his back to the fireplace. "I was five or six, I guess, and wanted to be a fireman. Mom bought this for me at a store in Whitefish. It was the ornament I always hung on the tree. My sister's was a stupid dancing bear and—"

"This one?" Cass held it out to him and he nodded, taking the little bear standing on her toes in ballet shoes and a ragged tutu.

"Yeah. She wanted to be a dancer." He snorted.

"Beth is so clumsy she trips over her own feet, but she was always trying to dance."

"Dreams are a good thing," Cass said quietly, trying not to shatter the moment.

"Yeah," he said, frowning as he looked at pieces of his past for another long moment before shifting his gaze to her again. She saw emotion crowd his eyes before he shuttered them and asked, "Where's Luke?"

Disappointment curled in the pit of her stomach. The chance for a deeper connection was lost as he stepped back behind the wall he kept between them. Even loving him wouldn't be enough to keep her here, Cass told herself. Not if he couldn't give. Bend. Not if he insisted on maintaining emotional distance from her.

"Sleeping," she said, letting go of the hurt wrapping itself around her heart. "Boston's lying under the crib. I swear that dog's better than a baby monitor. He lets me know instantly when Luke wakes up."

"Good. That's...good." He stared down at the ornaments in his hands and she could tell he was mentally miles away from this room. And her. He didn't want to open up with her, she knew that. But maybe if she pushed a little, at just the right time...

"Why'd you get him? Boston?"

He lifted his eyes to meet hers. A second ticked past. Then two. Then a few more, before he finally answered on a gusty sigh. "Because the house was too damn quiet after you left."

Warmth stole through her like a whispered breath. "You missed me."

Scowling, he set the ornaments back into the box with a gentleness that told her he still treasured those reminders of his past, whether he wanted to admit it or not. "Yeah. Didn't expect to. Wasn't happy about it. But yeah."

"I hoped you might call me, but you didn't."

He sighed. "Thought about it. A lot. I did miss you, though."

"I missed you, too." God, she had missed him. The sound of his taciturn voice. The heat of his body coiled around hers in the middle of the night. She'd missed hearing his boots on the hardwood floors. Missed seeing his hat hanging on a peg by the door. She'd missed the rare, treasured smiles he gave her and the way he fought against the tenderness that was a part of him. She'd missed everything about him.

His smile faded until his features were still and if she hadn't seen the suddenly churning emotions in his eyes, Cass might have thought he hadn't even heard her. "You should have called me, Cassie. About Luke. You should have called."

"I should have," she agreed and leaned closer, drawn to this man as she had never been drawn to another. But was that enough to build a lifetime on? Shared passion? Could she take that risk not only for herself, but for her son?

Jake leaned in, too, and then they were kissing and Cass's body lit up like the flickering lights ringing the room. She felt a blast of awareness sizzle through her system, trailing sparks through her bloodstream. She reached for him, linking her arms around his neck and holding on, as if afraid he would pull away, pull back.

She didn't have to worry about that, though. Jake drew her onto his lap, taking her mouth in deep, hungry gulps, as if he couldn't get enough of her. Their tongues tangled together, breath mingling, heartbeats racing in time as they each explored the other. Hands touched, caressed, pushed past the fabric denying them the feel of hot skin and found what they needed.

Strangling on the heavy beat of her own heart, Cass broke the kiss and gasped for breath as Jake's mouth closed on first one nipple, then the other. She didn't know where her shirt was. Didn't remember taking it off. Didn't care.

In seconds they were both naked and stretched out on the rug before the fire. Shadows danced and leaped on the walls. Outside, it was cold; inside, heat raged, claiming them, enveloping them both in a frantic sea of need and desire that was greater than anything else.

Touching, tasting, stroking, they moved together, skin sliding across skin, their tangled bodies creating more shadows on the walls. Jake swept one hand down to the blond curls at the center of her and when he stroked her hot, damp core, she arched off the floor, pushing into his hand.

"Jake, please," she whispered and heard her voice break unsteadily as she fought for air. It had been a nearly year and a half since he'd touched her, and she was ready to shatter already. Her body was eager to rocket off into the satiated oblivion she remembered so well.

"We've been apart too long," he whispered, dipping his head to kiss her, to run his tongue across her bottom lip. To nibble at her mouth while she whimpered and rocked her hips against him.

"We have. I can't wait. Don't want to wait." Gray eyes locked on blue. "Be in me," she said. "Be with me. Now, Jake."

"Now," he agreed and pushed his body into hers, sheathing himself so deeply that Cass gasped at the strength of his possession. She'd forgotten—or tried to forget—what it was like with Jake. How she lost herself in him. How her body became his. How he could make her want and feel so much more than she ever had before.

And now she had him inside her again and it was so right. So good. She wanted it to never end. She moved with him, and when he rolled over onto his back, she was astride him, taking him even deeper as she moved on him.

She watched the firelight play across his sculpted muscles. Watched her own hands stroke his skin and watched him squirm in response. He clenched his hands at her waist as he urged her into a faster pace. She rocked on him, throwing her head back, feeling like some wild warrior queen with him beneath her. And when her body trembled, letting her know the release was coming, she looked into his eyes, drowning in that deep, lake-blue.

She called his name as her body splintered and heard his hoarse shout moments later as he emptied himself into her.

When it was over, when her body was humming and replete, Cass slumped across Jake's chest and never wanted to move again.

"So," he whispered, waiting until she lifted her head to look at him. "Wrong time to ask, but you wouldn't be on the pill, would you?"

Her forehead hit his chest as the implications of that question slapped her. "No. I'm not."

"Doesn't matter," he said and that got her attention.

"Doesn't— What do you—how can it *not* matter?"

"We've got one kid. Would one more be so bad?"

Her heart hurt at the words. She'd always wanted a big family and in her mind, she could see her and Jake and the crowd of kids they would make living on this ranch. Plenty of room for children to run and they'd have horses and dogs and two parents who— didn't love each other? No. The dream images popped like soap bubbles.

How was it possible for her body to feel so good and her heart and mind to be steeped in misery? Propping herself up on her forearms, she looked down at him and shook her head. "We don't know what's going to happen between us, Jake. We can't go making another baby."

"Too late to worry about that now," he reminded her. "In fact, I hope you *are* pregnant."

Surprised, she blurted, "You can't be serious."

"Damn straight I am." He hooked one arm around her waist and rolled, pinning her beneath him. Looking down into her eyes, he said, "If you are, then this time I'll see my child grow in you. I'll be there when he's born—not hear about it five months later."

"And then what, Jake?" She shook her head slowly. "It wouldn't solve anything. It would just be more... complicated."

Jake's gaze shifted slightly and she wanted desperately to know what he was thinking, feeling. But the wall was up again and she was on the wrong side.

"Maybe," he said quietly, "but you'd have to stay here. With me. That, at least, would be settled."

She stared up at him for what felt like forever before saying, "Instead of just asking me to stay, you'd prefer to trap me. Or order me."

Scowling, he reminded her, "I asked you to marry me."

"You *told* me to marry you. There's a difference."

"You're trying to make this romantic. A love story," he muttered, and idly stroked a lock of her hair back from her face. "It's not, Cassie. It's two people who work well together finding common ground."

She caught his hand in hers and wished it was as easy to take hold of his heart. But looking into his eyes, she saw it was over. For her, it was done.

He wouldn't be what she needed. Wouldn't be the man he could be—just by opening his heart. So she couldn't stay. Couldn't risk him one day walking away as her father had done. Cass wouldn't put herself through that kind of loss again, and Luke would never know what it felt like to have his father turn his back and leave him behind.

She had to say it now, while she had the nerve. While she could force the words from her throat because the threat to her heart was so real. So immediate. "When the road's clear, I'm taking Luke and going back to Boston."

Jake went absolutely still. She felt her words hit him like stones because she saw pain in his eyes before he drew that so familiar shutter over what he was feeling.

"I won't let you go."

"Jake, you can't stop me." She touched his face because she could, her fingers tracing the stubble on his jaw. "I want what you can't give me. I love you, Jake."

He closed his eyes as if that would shut down his

hearing as well, and the pain of his reaction wound through her like barbed wire, tearing at her insides.

"I love you, but you won't love me," she said softly, willing those lake-blue eyes to open again. When they did, she said quietly, "So I can't stay."

"You love me," he said, gaze pinning hers. "But you'll still leave."

"One-sided love isn't going to work." God, did her voice sound as shaky as she felt? Could he hear her heart breaking?

He didn't see the truth. She wondered why, because it was all suddenly so clear to her.

"This, what we have? It's not enough, Jake. Not for me. Not for Luke. Heck, not even for you."

"That's where you're wrong," he said, arms tightening around her as if he could keep her there by sheer force of will. "I'll make it enough."

Ten

It would never be enough. Not with Cassie. Jake knew it. He just couldn't make himself admit it. Not to himself. Not to her.

Knowing she loved him gave him a sense of rightness he hadn't known in way too long. Knowing she was going to leave left him staring at a pool of darkness so complete he thought he would drown in it.

He knew what she wanted. What she needed. But he couldn't bring himself to comply. Doing that would lay everything on the line. Risk the life he'd built for himself. The peace he'd finally found.

Though if he were to be honest, he'd have to acknowledge that the so-called "peace" hadn't been the same since Cassie walked into his life.

He forked some hay into a stall, then moved along the line and did the same for the rest of the horses. It had always soothed him, these ordinary tasks. Usually, he let his mind wander while he did what needed doing as quickly as possible. Now though, he was taking his time because he was in no hurry to go back to the main house.

Yeah, he wanted to see Cassie. Hold her. Kiss her. But he didn't want to see the questions in her eyes. Didn't want to give her the chance to tell him again that she was leaving.

It had been three days since he'd watched her eyes as she told him she wouldn't stay. Three days and three nights and every one of those nights, they'd been together. Him, trying to show her what they could have if she'd back down; her, saying goodbye every time she touched him. He felt her pulling back, distancing herself from him in exactly the same way he had distanced himself from her since the beginning.

And it was damned hard to take.

Leaning on the handle of the pitchfork, he shot a quick look down the center aisle toward the open stable doors. The wind had eased off and it hadn't really snowed since yesterday. A couple more days like today and the roads would be clear and he'd have a hell of a time keeping her here. Where she and Luke belonged. He couldn't lose them. Either of them.

"Where's another damn blizzard when you need one?"

"Talking to yourself is never a good sign, son."

Jake turned to watch his grandfather approach. The older man was bundled up in his heavy coat, with his hat pulled down tight.

"At least when I talk to myself," Jake told him, forking more hay out for the horses, "I know I won't get a fight for my troubles."

"Won't you?" Ben snickered. "Isn't that what you're doing out here? Having a fight with yourself?"

Jake shot the older man a scowl that would have sent any of his employees running for cover. "Why do you have to be so perceptive?"

"The gift of age," Ben told him, leaning one arm on the top rail of a stall door. "Some things get harder, but you see everything around you a lot more clearly."

"Is that right?" Jake didn't want to have this conversation. All he wanted was some time to think. To plan. To find a way through the maze that lay stretched out in front of him.

"Like I can see plain as day that you're in love with Cassie."

Jake flinched, shook his head and tossed extra hay to one of the horses. "Nobody said anything about love."

"And that's a damn shame because if you can't say it, like as not, you'll lose it."

Jake's chest felt tight, as if there were an iron band squeezing his middle until his lungs could hardly draw air. Lose Cassie. He'd already lived without her once and didn't want to go back to the dark emptiness that his life had become in her absence.

But love? Love was dangerous. Love meant opening yourself to pain. Hadn't he had enough damn pain in his life already?

Ben stood there looking at him and Jake caught the sympathy in the older man's gaze. Rolling his shoulders, he shrugged off the pity and told himself he didn't want it. Didn't need it. He was in charge of his life and he wouldn't make apologies for the decisions he made. Even if those decisions cost him the one thing he wanted most.

"I had forty-nine years with your grandmother, Jake," Ben was saying softly, "and I wouldn't trade one moment of that time for all the treasure in the world."

Jake sighed at the reminder. His grandparents had the love story that most people only dreamed of, he knew that. Which was one of the reasons his spectacular failure with Lisa had torn the ground out from under his feet. He had expected the same kind of marriage. But maybe, he thought, he shouldn't have. He'd gone into that relationship too quickly, closing his eyes to who Lisa really was. Because he had *wanted* what his grandparents had shared. What his parents had found together before his father died.

When he didn't get it, Jake admitted silently, he'd shut down, refusing to try again. But who the hell could blame him? Lisa had made everyone's life a misery until she'd done him the supreme favor of leaving him. Hell, he'd take another tour of active duty in a war zone over going through that kind of marriage again.

Defensive, he asked, "Is there a point to this?"

"Yeah," Ben told him with a shake of his head. "The point is, don't be a jackass."

Jake snorted in spite of the thoughts racing through his mind. "Can always count on you to call it like you see it."

Ben sighed heavily and looked at him as if he were a huge disappointment, and Jake flinched under the uncomfortable feeling.

"You're a stubborn one. Always have been."

"Wonder where I got it?" Jake mused.

Snorting, Ben acknowledged, "Came by it naturally, that's for damn sure. Anyway, I'm here to tell you your mother wants to talk to you. She's on the phone in my place."

Jake was in no mood to talk to his mother. Her threat to take his son from Cassie was too fresh in his mind. "I'm busy."

"Jake…"

Stubborn, Jake reminded himself. His whole damn family was stubborn so it was pointless to try to avoid this call. His mother would only call back until she got hold of him. Best to just get it done now.

"Fine." He had a few things to say to her anyway. Maybe he could figure out just what she had been up to by threatening Cassie. That kind of move wasn't like his mother. She wasn't mean or vicious, so why even pretend to be willing to take Luke? There was something his mother wasn't telling him and now was as good a time as any to figure out what that was.

He leaned the pitchfork against the stable wall. "A man can't have five minutes to his damn self around this place. It's dogs and kids and women and grandfathers and now mothers."

Ben chuckled as Jake stomped out of the barn, and hearing that muffled laughter didn't improve Jake's mood any. Love. He wasn't in love. He was madly in *lust*, he knew that much for sure. But love wasn't something he was looking for.

Jake headed toward Ben's place and deliberately avoided looking at the main house. Once inside, Jake savored the warmth and tried to ignore the scent of pine that permeated the rooms. The power was back on and the Christmas tree lights shone brighter than ever, as if now that they were free of the generator, they were determined to light up at least this one small corner of the world.

His gaze drawn inevitably to the main house despite his efforts, he looked through the windows and pictured her inside. He knew that Cassie would have the lights she'd strung around the main room blazing. She was probably playing with Luke or maybe baking more Christmas cookies since he and the hands had eaten all of the batch she'd made the day before.

She'd made herself a part of this place. A part of *him*. And losing her was going to kill him.

Now in a particularly crappy mood, Jake snatched up the phone from beside his grandfather's favorite chair. "What is it, Mom?"

"Well, hello to you too," Elise Hunter said coolly. "And merry Christmas!"

His eyes rolled practically to the back of his head. The whole family knew he didn't do Christmas, yet none of them stopped trying. "Right. Same to you. What's up?"

"Do you think you might be able to speak to me without trying to bite my head off?"

Sighing, Jake yanked off his hat and scraped one hand through his hair. "A week ago, you threatened to take my son from his mother and now you're surprised that I'm a little testy?"

She laughed and the sound was so familiar, it eased some of the heaviness he felt inside.

"Oh, Jake. I was never going to take Luke from Cassie."

"What?" Frowning, he fixed his gaze blindly on his grandfather's tree, spots of bright red and green and blue blurring weirdly into a kaleidoscope of color. "What do you mean? You threatened Cassie. That's why she ran to me in the first place."

"You're welcome."

"What?"

Her laughter faded away and drowned in a sigh of frustration. In his mind, he could see her, sitting at the desk that had once been his father's with a wide window and a view of Boston at her back.

"Jake, I would never take your son. I was only trying to force Cassie's hand. Once her sister told me about Luke, was I supposed to just sit quietly and pretend I didn't know?"

His frown deepened as his fist tightened around the phone.

"Would you rather I'd done nothing?" she prodded, her insistence demanding an answer. "Would you rather not know about Luke at all?"

"No," he said abruptly. The thought of not knowing about Luke's existence hit him hard. Not ever seeing the boy? Never feeling his solid weight in his arms? Not seeing that wide, drooly smile, hearing his crow of laughter?

If Cassie left, Jake wouldn't see his son's first steps. Wouldn't hear his first word. Wouldn't teach him to ride a horse or to make a snow fort. He wouldn't show Luke the best fishing spots on the mountain and he wouldn't be a part of his own son's day-to-day life. He'd miss everything, big and small, and that knowledge tore at him, leaving Jake cringing from the pain.

That emptiness was back inside him again at the thought of not having Luke in his life. And Cassie. Without her, what the hell did he have? An empty house? A lonely ranch? He nearly choked on the thought of another fifty or so years of life spent without her laughter. Without her touch.

"Jake," his mother said softly, "don't let this chance with Cassie slip away."

Is that what he was doing? Was he really going to allow her to leave and try to pretend it didn't matter?

"I know, the hermit on the mountain doesn't want to hear that he's not invincible on his own."

Jake reached out and flicked his finger against a candy cane on the tree, sending it swinging. "I'm not a hermit."

"And you're not invincible," Elise said quietly. "Jake, Cassie loves you. Her sister told me."

"I know," he muttered, gaze fixed on that twist of red and white peppermint as if it meant his life. "I know that."

"I think you care for her, too," his mother continued.

"Of course I care," he told her hotly. "What am I, made of stone?"

"Have you bothered to tell her that?" She waited for him to say something and when he didn't, she sighed again. "Of course you haven't. Jake, I'm your mother and I love you. So I'm going to tell you that if you lose this chance at happiness, you'll never forgive yourself."

He dropped his hat onto Ben's chair, scrubbed one hand across his face and wished he could just hang up. But ending the conversation wouldn't stop any of the thoughts charging through his mind.

"Have you forgotten Lisa?"

She laughed. "That would be hard to do," his mother said. "That woman caused more problems—wait a minute." Her voice went low and hard. "Are you saying that's why you've shut out your family and any chance at love? Because you made a mistake with Lisa?"

"Doesn't that make sense?" he demanded, trying to defend himself and his actions. Though hearing his mother say it out loud made him sound profoundly stupid. "I married her, didn't I? My mistake, and it was a big one."

"Yes, it was." Elise sighed a little and he heard the love in her voice when she said, "But you learn from a mistake and move on. Jake, Cassie isn't Lisa, and you're doing a disservice to both of you if you can't see that. Cassie deserves better and frankly honey, so do you."

Well, hell. Oh, he could admit that right from the beginning, he'd been waiting for Cassie to somehow morph into Lisa. To become demanding and complaining. But she hadn't. She'd more than proven herself, yet apparently there was still some small part of him that didn't believe.

"I know she's not Lisa." He did. Jake had seen that for himself during the first week she was here, and he'd seen it again after she showed up with Luke. Cassie had made a place for herself here. She had friends on the ranch. She knew how to work and wasn't afraid to step in and do what needed doing.

Yes, he'd been waiting for her to fail. To prove to him that she couldn't handle ranch life. But she hadn't. Not once. She did what was needed and more. And she did it with a smile. Unlike Lisa, Cassie didn't complain about the ranch being so far from "civilization." Hell, she didn't complain about much of anything.

Frowning, he did silent battle with his own feelings. Want fought against caution. Need scuffled with fear.

Fear?

Jake wasn't a man who admitted to being afraid. Not on the battlefield. Not when he was caught in a blizzard. Nothing shook him—well, nothing *had* until Cassie.

"I knew if I threatened to take Luke from her, Cassie would go to you," Elise was saying, and Jake struggled to focus. "I hoped that you two would find a way to work out what was keeping you apart."

"It's not that easy," he whispered.

"It could be if you let it," his mother argued. "Jake, I love you. But you're a fool if you let this chance at the family you always wanted get away from you."

When his mother hung up, Jake stayed right where he was, thinking. Surrounded by the scents and sights of Christmas, he pulled up mental images of Cassie and lost himself in them. Her, smiling up at him. Her, rising over him in the night, taking him into her body and holding him there. Cassie playing with Luke. Cassie working alongside the men to clear snowdrifts, and still finding the time to pack a few snowballs and get a war started to break up the tedium of the work.

Cassie laughing. Cassie sleeping beside him. Cassie sitting on the floor of the main room, pieces of long past Christmases scattered around her.

His heart ached and his head pounded. Misery settled on his shoulders and he couldn't shake it off. Maybe he didn't deserve to. Maybe Cassie was a gift and because he'd been too stupid to see it, he was destined to lose her and the family they might have made, leaving misery as his only companion.

And if what they had ended, it would be his fault.

Cassie hadn't failed. He had. Through his own reluctance to try again.

And didn't that make him a coward? Instinctively, he turned from that word, but it was, he told himself, the only one that fit.

He looked out the window again at the house across the yard. Draped in snow, blurred lamplight was the only thing he could see through the treated windows. His woman and his child were in that house.

Was he going to fail them?

Hell no.

"It's not enough, Claudia." Cass sat on the window seat in Jake's bedroom. He was out on the ranch somewhere and Luke was downstairs with Anna. They'd let her sleep in today and though she appreciated the thought, she hated sleeping away what little time she had left at the ranch.

"Cass," her sister said quietly, "you've got to stop judging all men by Dad's sterling example."

"Easy to say," Cass murmured, watching the guys plowing paths through the snow. The sky was blue, the wind was still, and she knew that if the weather held, she'd be leaving in a few days.

Her heart ached at the thought, but what choice did she have?

"You've only been there a week, Cass. Are you really ready to give up so easily? I thought you loved him."

Stung, Cass frowned. "I do love him. And I'm not giving up, I'm just accepting reality rather than waiting around for it to bite me in the butt."

"Right." Claudia blew out a breath in exasperation.

"You've spent most of my life telling me to stand up for myself. To acknowledge what I want and go after it. To not let anything get in my way."

"Yes, so?"

"So, you want the cowboy!" Claudia's voice went sharp. "And you're not willing to stay and fight for him."

"How can I?" Cass lowered her voice and leaned her forehead against the cold glass pane. Looking down into the yard, she watched the cowboys, all bundled up in their hats and coats, and searched for Jake. She didn't see him out there and she frowned in disappointment.

Even knowing that she was leaving, he clung to the taciturn, stoic cowboy image rather than show her the man he kept locked away. Why wouldn't he let her in before it was too late? And how was she going to live without him in her life?

"Unless he loves me, there's no guarantee he won't one day just walk away."

"There's no guarantee anyway," Claudia pointed out.

"Good pep talk. Thanks."

Claudia laughed a little. "Who knew love could be such a gigantic pain?"

"Wait until it's your turn," Cass warned.

"Please. I'm nineteen. Talk to me when I'm thirty."

"Fine." Cass leaned back against the wall, keeping her gaze on the wide sweep of blue sky and the snow-tipped evergreens standing around the edge of the lake far below. "Look, I just wanted to let you know that once the road clears, I'll be coming home."

"Uh-huh." Claudia huffed out a breath. "Cass, you

said Jake wants you to marry him. To stay there on that ranch you told us about so often you bored us to tears. He wants you to be pregnant again."

That all sounded great in the abstract, Cass thought, wishing her sister could understand. But maybe that was impossible. Claudia had been only ten when their father walked out on them. And because Cass and Dave had been there for her, her life really hadn't been interrupted. It was Cass who remembered the devastation left in her father's wake.

"But he won't—"

"Cass, sweetie," Claudia cut in, "you do realize that *you're* the one walking away, right?"

That one quiet sentence slammed home like a thunderclap. She sat straight up as if jerked into place by invisible strings. Was that what she was doing? Was she running first to keep from being left behind? Had she so little faith that the only way to protect herself was to leave before Jake could?

"Oh my God. You're right."

"That just never gets old," Claudia murmured on a heartfelt sigh.

Cass hardly heard her. Thoughts racing, heart pounding, stomach spinning, she inched off the window seat and started pacing. "Funny, I never saw it like that, Claud. I just want to make sure Luke's protected. Safe."

And me, too, she thought but didn't say aloud. *I want me to be safe, too.* She couldn't bear it if Jake walked away from her. If he turned his back on her and their children. So what had she done instead? She'd given up to avoid being hurt.

"Of course you want to protect Luke," Claudia

agreed. "But maybe you could give his father more of a chance to figure this out? I mean, you've had Luke and the knowledge of him for nearly a year and a half. Jake's had what? A week or so?"

"True." Cass looked out the window and still didn't see Jake. Where was he? She had to talk to him. "I've gotta go find Jake, Claud. I'll call you later."

She dropped the cell phone onto the bed and hurried out of the room and down the long second-story hallway. She didn't notice the rugs on the bamboo flooring or the family photos and paintings dotting the walls. Taking the stairs quickly, she made a turn to go to the kitchen and ask Anna to watch Luke for a little longer, but something in the great room caught her eye and dragged her to a stop.

A Christmas tree.

The biggest, most beautiful tree she'd ever seen sat square in front of the windows, lights bursting from every branch. Heart in her throat, Cass walked hesitantly into the room and then stopped dead again when Jake, with Luke perched on one arm, stepped out from behind the tree and smiled at her.

Jake was nervous.

Hell, he hadn't been nervous since the night he left for boot camp. But he had the warm, solid weight of his son on his arm and the scent of Christmas filling his lungs, so he fought past that flutter of nerves and started talking.

He'd have felt better if Cassie would smile at him, but she looked so dumbfounded, he figured that wasn't going to happen.

"I went out and got us a tree."

Nodding, she whispered, "I see that. It's beautiful."

They were talking like strangers and it was his fault, Jake told himself silently. He'd spent so much damn time keeping her out, that now she wasn't even trying to get in anymore.

But screw that, it couldn't be too late.

"Luke and I decorated it," he said and grinned as his son patted his cheek.

"Nice job. Jake…"

"I went out this morning to get the tree." He glanced at it now, saw its beauty, and wondered why he had avoided this season and the miracle of it for so long. Shifting his gaze back to her, he said, "I cut myself off from a lot of things over the years and it took you and Luke to remind me of all I've been missing."

"Why, Jake?" Her gaze locked with his. "Can you tell me *why* you stopped celebrating Christmas?"

He hitched Luke a little higher, smoothed one hand over the baby's soft hair and took a breath. It wouldn't be easy, but he was through holding back. It was time to take a chance. He told her about that long-ago Christmas Eve on a battlefield and as he did, he relived it himself. The smells, the sounds, the awful silence when the attack was over and his friends lay broken in the sand.

When he looked at her again, he saw tears shining in her eyes, and had to force words past the knot in his throat. "When those guys died, I think something in me did, too."

"Oh Jake, I'm so sorry."

He blew out a breath, looked at the tree, then looked to her again. "I used that night as an excuse to pull back. Just like I used Lisa to keep you at bay. Didn't really see that clearly enough until today. But I see it now. I know what's important. *Who's* important."

Walking toward her, he kept his gaze fixed on hers and kept a tight grip on their son, until Luke leaned out and reached for his mother. As Cassie folded Luke into her arms, Jake stared at the two of them for a long minute. "You two are everything to me, Cassie. *You* are everything to me."

Shaking her head and blinking back tears, she said, "I can't believe you went out in chest-high drifts of snow to get a Christmas tree."

"Yeah, well," he said with a quick grin and a shrug, "you wanted one and Luke deserves one. And me?" He shot a look at the tree over his shoulder and felt years of pain and loneliness and misery slide from him in the soft glow of way too many lights. Looking back at Cassie, he said, "I wanted this tree because this is our first Christmas together. As a family."

"Oh, Jake…"

He reached out and pulled her and Luke into the center of his arms. "And I need you to know that I don't want this to be our *last* Christmas together." Bending his head, he kissed her gently, then dropped a kiss on Luke's forehead.

"I want it all, Cassie," he said, his gaze moving over her features like a caress. "I want kids and dogs and noise and chaos. I want that life we could build together. Marry me, Cassie. Marry me because I love you. Because I'm no damn good without you."

She gasped in a breath and a solitary tear fell and tracked down her cheek.

"Marry me because we deserve to be happy. And we will be. I swear it to you." He looked into fog-gray eyes and saw a future shining there that he never would have believed possible until he'd met her. "Marry me and I swear, every day will be Christmas."

She laughed a little, choking on the tears clogging her throat. How was it possible, Cassie wondered, to be so sad and lonely one minute and have the world offered to you in the next?

Her gaze slid to the massive Christmas tree and she thought about him riding out in the aftermath of the storm just so she wouldn't be disappointed. Just to make her happy. To prove he loved her.

Staring up into his eyes, Cassie knew this man would never walk away from his family. He would always be there for her. He would always come through—even if it meant pushing through eight feet of snow. He was a better man than her father had ever been, and she would never doubt him again.

"You haven't said yes yet," Jake told her, draping one arm around her shoulders and steering her toward their first Christmas tree. "So let me give you your present."

"Present?" Cassie laughed. The man was full of surprises.

Scooping Luke into his arms, Jake handed Cassie a small hand-carved box from under the tree. When she opened it, her heart melted. Nestled inside was an antique ring. Gold with several tiny diamonds and one opal in the center, it was lovely. "Oh, Jake."

"It was my grandmother's," he said, lifting the ring from its nest to slide onto her left ring finger.

"But I can't—"

He kissed her quick and light, then gave her a smile that lit up all the old shadows in his eyes, shattering them forever. "I want you to have it. So does Pop. This ring has a history of a lot of love," he told her. "I want to build on that love with you."

Outside was snow and cold. Inside was firelight, Christmas lights and more warmth than Cassie had ever felt before.

Jake cupped her cheek in his palm. "Tell me you still love me and that the answer is yes. Marry me, Cassie. Don't leave me alone on the mountain."

Her heart was so full it was hard to breathe, and Cassie simply didn't care. If she could freeze this one moment in time she would, because it was perfect and she wanted it to last forever. Yet even as she thought it, she knew their future was going to be just as wonderful and she couldn't wait to get started on it.

"Yes, Jake, always yes. I love you so much."

"Thank God," he whispered, kissing her again before pulling her against him.

And in the soft glow of Christmas, fresh promises were born.

Epilogue

One year later

"Me do it, Daddy!" Luke jumped up and down until his father picked him up and held him high enough that he could put the little fire engine ornament as close to the star at the top of the tree as possible. When he was finished, the little boy turned a wide grin on his father. "Fire truck onna tree!"

"You bet." Jake laughed, gave his son a hug, then set him down to race through the house with Boston—probably headed for the kitchen.

"Oh, Jake, that baby is the cutest thing I've ever seen," his mother said, coming down the stairs from the nursery.

"You mean since me, of course," Jake teased.

"She means, since *me,*" his sister interrupted from

her spot curled up on the couch. Beth, her husband and kids were here for Christmas along with Cassie's sister Claudia and her brother Dave and his family.

It was a full house and Jake was enjoying every minute of it. What a difference a year made, he told himself as he smiled at his grandfather, sitting in a chair by the fire, reading to Beth's youngest.

Not only did Jake have Cassie and two amazing kids, but he had his own family back in his life as well. The mountain wasn't as lonely as it used to be, and he thanked heaven for it every night.

"Cassie asked me to send you upstairs," his mother said as she went up on her toes to kiss his cheek.

"Everything all right?" Instant worry shot through him and he knew that it would always be like that. When a man had a lot in his life—he had a lot to lose.

"Fine, worrier. She's out of baby wipes and she wants you to bring her some from the storage room in the basement."

"Okay. That I can do." He turned toward his mission, but his mother stopped him with one hand on his arm.

"I can't tell you what it means to me to see you so happy."

He kissed her forehead. "You don't have to. Now that I have kids, I finally get it."

"Good." She pushed him away, called out to Beth's husband to pour her some wine and then told Jake, "Go. Don't make your wife wait."

Smiling to himself, Jake went to the basement, got a couple boxes of wipes, then headed back upstairs. As he went, he looked into the great room at his extended family. There were lights and candles and cookies and wreaths and a gigantic tree and damned if it all didn't look perfect.

From the kitchen came the amazing scents of a roasting turkey and the sounds of Anna sneaking Luke an extra cookie that Jake was sure would be shared with Boston. Claudia was in the study on the phone with one of her friends and Dave and his wife were out in the stables while their kids napped upstairs. Anna was in her glory with so many kids to look after, and she kept sending parents out of the room so she could have as much fun as she wanted to.

With the noise of a stereo playing Christmas carols and conversations rising and falling, Jake shook his head and took the stairs two at a time. He went directly to the nursery beside the master bedroom.

Pausing on the threshold just to watch his wife and child, Jake knew he would never get enough of this view. Cassie sat in a flowered rocker, nursing their daughter as snow fell softly outside the window. A small lamp beside the chair threw pale, golden light across his girls. When Cassie heard him, she looked up and smiled and everything inside Jake went completely still.

She was his everything.

"How's our girl doing?" he asked, walking into the room to squat down in front of the rocker.

"Rachel is almost finished with her dinner, aren't you, sweet girl?"

He'd had his wish and spent nine months watching Cassie grow with their child and he'd loved every minute of it. Labor and delivery were tougher than he would have imagined, but he learned again just how strong his wife was. She was already talking about having another one, and Rachel was only three months old. That was fine with Jake, though. They both wanted a big family.

The baby gurgled, gave a milky smile, then reached out and grabbed hold of Jake's finger, curling her tiny fingers around his. His heart squeezed painfully and as he dropped a kiss onto the baby's forehead, he looked up at Cassie. Briefly he remembered his life before the chaos, when peace was all-important and silence ruled his days and nights. He couldn't even understand the man he used to be. He was simply grateful that man was gone.

Looking into fog-gray eyes, he whispered, "Thank you for saving the loner on the mountain."

"Merry Christmas, Jake."

* * * * *

If you liked THE COWBOY'S PRIDE AND JOY, check out USA Today bestselling author Maureen Child's other BILLIONAIRES & BABIES stories!

HAVE BABY, NEED BILLIONAIRE DOUBLE THE TROUBLE

Available now, from Harlequin Desire!

If you liked this BILLIONAIRES & BABIES novel, watch for the next book in this Number 1 bestselling Desire series, THE MISSING HEIR by Barbara Dunlop, available December 2014.

#2341 THE SECRET AFFAIR
The Westmorelands • by Brenda Jackson
Facing her family's disapproval, Jillian ended her affair with Dr. Aidan Westmoreland. But he knows their passion won't be denied—not for secrets or mistakes. And he'll follow her around the world to prove it...

#2342 PREGNANT BY THE TEXAN
Texas Cattleman's Club: After the Storm • by Sara Orwig
When Stella discovers she's pregnant from one passionate night with Aaron, she declines his dutiful marriage proposal. But the Dallas mogul lost one family already; he doesn't intend to lose this child—or Stella!

#2343 THE MISSING HEIR
Billionaires and Babies • by Barbara Dunlop
When tragedy struck, Amber took care of Cole's infant half brother. Yet a custody battle soon forces Cole to claim the child...and lie to the woman he can't seem to resist. Will he ever win Amber's trust?

#2344 CHRISTMAS IN THE BILLIONAIRE'S BED
The Kavanaghs of Silver Glen • by Janice Maynard
English beauty Emma broke Aidan Kavanagh's heart a decade ago. Now she's back—as a guest at his brother's Christmas wedding! Will the truth about her betrayal heal old wounds, or will she lose Aidan all over again?

#2345 SCANDALOUSLY EXPECTING HIS CHILD
The Billionaires of Black Castle • by Olivia Gates
Reclaiming his heritage means everything to Ralden Kuroshiro, until his passion for Scarlett Delacroix threatens all of his plans...and her life. Will he give up everything he thought he wanted to keep her and his baby?

#2346 HER UNFORGETTABLE ROYAL LOVER
Duchess Diaries • by Merline Lovelace
Undercover agent Dominic St. Sebastian learns he's technically a royal duke. But when the woman who discovered his heritage is attacked, leaving her with amnesia, it seems the only person the bewildered beauty remembers is him... _____

REQUEST YOUR FREE BOOKS!
2 FREE NOVELS PLUS 2 FREE GIFTS!

H HARLEQUIN® *Desire*

ALWAYS POWERFUL, PASSIONATE AND PROVOCATIVE

YES! Please send me 2 FREE Harlequin Desire® novels and my 2 FREE gifts (gifts are worth about $10). After receiving them, if I don't wish to receive any more books, I can return the shipping statement marked "cancel." If I don't cancel, I will receive 6 brand-new novels every month and be billed just $4.55 per book in the U.S. or $4.99 per book in Canada. That's a savings of at least 13% off the cover price! It's quite a bargain! Shipping and handling is just 50¢ per book in the U.S. and 75¢ per book in Canada.* I understand that accepting the 2 free books and gifts places me under no obligation to buy anything. I can always return a shipment and cancel at any time. Even if I never buy another book, the two free books and gifts are mine to keep forever.

225/326 HDN F4ZC

Name	(PLEASE PRINT)
Address	Apt. #
City	State/Prov.	Zip/Postal Code

Signature (if under 18, a parent or guardian must sign)

Mail to the **Harlequin® Reader Service:**
IN U.S.A.: P.O. Box 1867, Buffalo, NY 14240-1867
IN CANADA: P.O. Box 609, Fort Erie, Ontario L2A 5X3

Want to try two free books from another line?
Call 1-800-873-8635 or visit www.ReaderService.com.

* Terms and prices subject to change without notice. Prices do not include applicable taxes. Sales tax applicable in N.Y. Canadian residents will be charged applicable taxes. Offer not valid in Quebec. This offer is limited to one order per household. Not valid for current subscribers to Harlequin Desire books. All orders subject to credit approval. Credit or debit balances in a customer's account(s) may be offset by any other outstanding balance owed by or to the customer. Please allow 4 to 6 weeks for delivery. Offer available while quantities last.

Your Privacy—The Harlequin® Reader Service is committed to protecting your privacy. Our Privacy Policy is available online at www.ReaderService.com or upon request from the Harlequin Reader Service.

We make a portion of our mailing list available to reputable third parties that offer products we believe may interest you. If you prefer that we not exchange your name with third parties, or if you wish to clarify or modify your communication preferences, please visit us at www.ReaderService.com/consumerschoice or write to us at Harlequin Reader Service Preference Service, P.O. Box 9062, Buffalo, NY 14269. Include your complete name and address.

HD13R

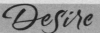
Here's a sneak peek of
THE SECRET AFFAIR
by New York Times *and* USA TODAY *bestselling author*
Brenda Jackson

Dr. Aidan Westmoreland entered his apartment and removed his lab coat. After running a hand down his face, he glanced at his watch, frustrated. He'd hoped he would have heard something by now. What if…

The ringing of his cell phone made him pause. It was the call he'd been waiting for. "Paige?"

"Yes, it's me."

"Is Jillian still going?" he asked, not wasting time with chitchat.

There was a slight pause on the other end, and in that short space of time knots formed in his stomach. "Yes, she's still going on the cruise, Aidan."

He released the breath he'd been holding as Paige continued, "Jill still has no idea I'm aware that the two of you had an affair."

Aidan hadn't known Paige knew the truth either, until she'd paid him a surprise visit last month. According to her, she'd figured things out the year Jillian had entered medical school. She'd become suspicious when he'd come home for his cousin Riley's wedding and she'd overheard him call Jillian Jilly in an intimate tone. Paige had been concerned this past year when she'd noticed

Jillian seemed troubled by something that she wouldn't share with Paige.

Paige had talked to Ivy, Jillian's best friend, who'd also been concerned about Jillian. Ivy had shared everything about the situation with Paige. Which had prompted Paige to fly to Charlotte and confront him. Until then, Aidan had been clueless as to the real reason behind his and Jillian's breakup.

When Paige had told him about the cruise she and Jillian had planned and she'd suggested an idea for getting Jillian on the cruise alone, he'd readily embraced it.

"I've done my part and the rest is up to you, Aidan. I hope you can convince Jill of the truth."

Moments later he ended the call and continued to the kitchen, where he grabbed a beer. Two weeks on the open seas with Jillian would be interesting. But he intended to make it more than just interesting. He aimed to make it productive.

A determined smile spread across his lips. By the time the cruise ended there would be no doubt in Jillian's mind that he was the only man for her.

Find out how this secret affair began—and how Aidan plans to claim his woman in THE SECRET AFFAIR by New York Times and USA TODAY bestselling author Brenda Jackson.

Available December 2014, wherever Harlequin® Desire books and ebooks are sold!

HARLEQUIN®

Desire

ALWAYS POWERFUL, PASSIONATE AND PROVOCATIVE.

USA TODAY bestselling author
Sara Orwig

Brings you the next installment of
Texas Cattleman's Club: After the Storm

PREGNANT BY THE TEXAN

Available December 2014

When folks think of Stella Daniels, they think
unassuming, even plain. But after a devastating
tornado hits Royal, Texas, Stella steps up and leads the
recovery effort. That's when she attracts the attention of
construction magnate Aaron Nichols—and a surprising
night of passion ensues.

Aaron sees something special in the no-nonsense
admin, and he's more than happy to bring her out of
her shell. But when he discovers Stella's expecting his
child, can he overcome his demons to be the hero this
hometown heroine really needs?

Don't miss other exciting titles from the
Texas Cattleman's Club: After the Storm:

STRANDED WITH THE RANCHER
by Janice Maynard

SHELTERED BY THE MILLIONAIRE
by Catherine Mann

Available wherever books and ebooks are sold.

HARLEQUIN®

Desire

ALWAYS POWERFUL, PASSIONATE AND PROVOCATIVE.

USA TODAY bestselling author

Janice Maynard

Brings you the next installment of
The Kavanaghs of Silver Glen

CHRISTMAS IN THE BILLIONAIRE'S BED

Available December 2014

'Tis the season for a steamy reunion for past lovers...

Whatever possessed Emma Braithwaite to move
to Silver Glen? She had no illusions that being in
Aidan Kavanagh's hometown would reignite their
love. But now that Aidan's returned for his brother's
Christmas wedding, it's clear her explosive attraction
to him has lost none of its power.

She is the cool English beauty whose betrayal once
shattered his heart. So Aidan's not looking for
reconciliation—all he wants is Emma in his bed!
Needless to say, Emma has other ideas: she's not settling
for anything less than commitment this time...

Don't miss other exciting titles from Janice Maynard's
The Kavanaghs of Silver Glen:

BABY FOR KEEPS
A NOT-SO-INNOCENT SEDUCTION

Available wherever books and ebooks are sold.

HD733576